Songs My Mother Taught Me

Songs My Mother Taught Me

A Novel

Eva Izsak

SHE WRITES PRESS

Published 2024
Printed in the United States of America
Print ISBN: 978-1-64742-698-9
E-ISBN: 978-1-64742-699-6
Library of Congress Control Number: 2024905800

For information, address:
She Writes Press
1569 Solano Ave #546
Berkeley, CA 94707

Interior Design by Kiran Spees

She Writes Press is a division of SparkPoint Studio, LLC.

To my departed

Songs my mother taught me
In the days long vanished;
Seldom from her eyelids
Were the teardrops banished.
Now I teach my children,
Each melodious measure.
Oft the tears are flowing,
Oft they flow from my memory's treasure.

— *Adolf Heyduk*
(English lyrics by Natalia Macfarren)

Part I

VARIATIONS

Prologue

December 13

Earlier this evening, I told you, *"You are dying."* No one dared tell you the truth before, and I cooperated with the lie. Belatedly, you insisted on being taken to an exclusive, private hospital to see whether surgery could still save you. No one dared telling you it is futile. That your body, all skin and bones, is too frail for any doctor to attempt touching it with a knife. If there ever was something to be done about the cancer so gently gnawing at your internal organs—well, now it is too late.

The last couple of months have seen a rapid deterioration to the point that you no longer crave food; your failing body is unable to process it. You are down to a yogurt a day and some tea. This cannot go on for much longer.

We had always been one. With no barriers between us, you could easily see through the lies. Without understanding exactly why, you hated me for them. You hissed and cussed in blind frustration. So I stopped. This time, on our daily telephone call, I finally told you there was no point in all that poking and *probing and examinations, transferring you by ambulance from here to there, hospital beds, needles, and tubes. I don't want any of that for you. Neither do you. All we can hope for is a quiet end, in your own bed.*

And I told you, "I will not leave you. We will be together."

You listened calmly. You carefully considered my analysis and after a brief reflection agreed with the conclusion.

You said, "So it is all settled now. I am at peace."

And then you added, "This will be my final joy. Spending the last days of my life with you. Our last shared hours of happiness." As if we were heading toward some relaxing vacation in a luxurious spa, to be cuddled in warmth and leisure. Something to look forward to. You then said goodbye and gently replaced the receiver.

We start the final leg of our journey. A journey within a journey. I am packing my suitcase. I hesitate whether or not to take a dress suitable for a funeral. The thought feels obscene. But I do. I dread booking the flight that will take me closer to your death. But I do. I know this is a voyage we have to take. Just the two of us. And I will accompany you as far as I am allowed to go.

Four years ago, the head of the oncology department at the hospital gave you no more than three months.

"Does she have, perhaps, six?" I tried.

"Now you are bargaining with me," he replied, with the arrogance of God.

You defied God before. You fought numerous battles with Him, always ending up with the upper hand. We had a few "false alarms" over the years (a mass discovered in your left breast, thrombosis in your lungs). We parted at airports, fearing we might never see each other again, said final goodbyes, waved all the way to passport control. I cried throughout those flights.

Then you pulled through. Because you knew I still needed you.

For you are still the only one able to comfort me. Nothing has changed since I was a month-old babe rocked in your arms, cuddled at your bosom. If anything, you have gained confidence and become even better at it. You are the engine that powers my existence.

The current crisis seems like just one more episode in our long-running soap opera.

Only this time there is no escape.

Mama. We begin our goodbye. A simultaneous death and birth. I still do not know where you end and where I begin. We must undergo the intricate surgery that will define those borders and forever sever us from one another. I am over fifty. You are dying. It's time to cut the umbilical cord.

This story will end with your death.

Before I Was

Rural Transylvania, early 1930s

Before I was, you were alone. I wasn't there the first thirty-five years. I only joined for the latter leg of the journey—the "easy" segment, one could argue. Before I was, you had to fend for yourself. You don't talk about it. To translate those events into words would wake them from their entombment, and you can't take that risk. So I have to rely on the tidbits you let drop while I was playing at your feet on the bare tile kitchen floor. Almost absentmindedly, to keep me from distracting you while sprinkling the right amount of paprika into a pot of goulash bubbling on the stove, you tossed a few shreds of memory my way. You regretted your half-hearted generosity as soon as the pungent vapors filled the air, together with the stream of my follow-up questions, bombarding you with childish curiosity. You tasted the slushy stew, pursed your lips, and replied with an impatient wave of your hand, as if chasing away a persistent fly. But a crack had already gaped in the crust of the earth, letting a faint scent of noxious magma escape, mixing with the fragrant odors of lunch being prepared. Your eyes glazed—within a split second, my warm mommy transformed into someone I did not recognize. The beasts stirred in their deep caves, and you were forcing them back, wielding your wooden spoon, flapping your arms, beating the air, piling up whatever came to hand—the cupboard, the kitchen table, the refrigerator—to block their entry. An inquisitive six-year-old redhead, I still knew better than to insist. Gagged, eager to reverse my gaffe, I joined my tiny hands to the effort, rolled over dolls, toys, and offered childish hugs to force the past back; to keep you safe from the beast's fingers stretched out to grab and pull you away from me.

Decades later, I am left with nothing but those decaying morsels I managed to save from your sweeping broom—always at hand tidying up the mess—to piece together a puzzle that is missing more than it holds.

I want to tell your story. I want to give you the voice you never had. There are a thousand ways for a story to emerge from its cocoon. How do I find the right one? I dig for faraway clues.

Session 1

Names

What do I call you? I must have started with "Mama." Don't all babies? But then I guess you became *Anyu*—the Hungarian word for mother. And all the diminutives that are imperative to Eastern European languages: *Anyukam*, my mother, and *Anyucikam*, my little mother. When did you become *Ima*, the plain Hebrew word for mother? Probably after I started school. We stayed with it. The original *Anyu* was later used by your grandchildren for "Grandma," a twist that met with your approval. The title and image of a grandmother could never fit with your coquettishness.

I have no difficulty recalling what you called me. It was never by my name. To this day, when you pick up the phone and recognize my voice—provided you are not in one of those foul moods of yours—you most often utter a cheerful *gyongy viragom*—plainly, "my pearl flower." Or sometimes *csilag fenyem*—my starlight, or *kincsem*—my treasure. Names out of a Chinese novel or images of a Native American chief smoking his pipe under a starry sky, perhaps? To my ears, all these are as natural as "Tom" or "Sarah." I hear these terms of endearment and feel protected in your timeless embrace. When you are gone, I will be a pearl flower no more.

Then there is the "other" you: the one picking up the phone, her voice as shrill as chalk on a blackboard. I neglect calling for a day or two and inevitably encounter the bitter tone coupled with condescending sarcasm:

"Oh, you *finally* remembered you still have a mother? That I am not quite dead yet?"

Or you leave a ten-minute message on my answering machine, accusing me of screening your calls, of being a neglectful, selfish daughter, threatening me with the wrath of God. When I call back, trying to mend the rupture, you hang up. You complain of loneliness while your granddaughters are unwelcome in your apartment for fear that they may be carrying in some sand from the beach, stomping with their "big, dirty feet" on your meticulously vacuumed carpets.

This cleanliness malady is not new. One of the few anecdotes you did share with me about life in the concentration camps—what still mattered to you even in that hell, your claim to triumph—was staying clean.

"I was the only inmate in our barrack not to have been afflicted with lice. I would pick them out one by one all night long until there were none left," you boasted as you plucked one in a swift motion from my head.

"Oh, it's a big one. You must've acquired it at school."

I looked up, finding it hard to believe that my immaculate mother, with her spotless home, knew what lice looked like.

"I washed even then, in the freezing winter, using snow to cleanse myself," you continued, illustrating your coup.

I don't even dare to hand you a slice of bread from the basket for fear you may not be willing to eat it once touched.

Am I conducting some sort of a belated "accounting" with you? Is this an accusatory proclamation? Absolutely not. It would have been a cruel and futile endeavor at your age. I am just trying to better understand how we got here. How the endless love and adoration morphed into an obligatory daily telephone call during which I don't even listen to you.

Over the years, I have noticed that I am becoming more and more *you*. I am discovering you under my skin and fingernails. I always considered myself "Daddy's girl." His easy rolling laughter, his muscles, the sweet smell of cigarettes, something light and sunny about him—he was a much more compelling model to emulate. Other than when encountering his thunderous temper to which I, the apple of his eye, was mercifully immune. I willingly identified with him. Truth be told, I am somewhat disappointed to find you in me. Compared with my father's soaring image, you painted a pitiful picture: sour-faced, ill-humored, hurried, agitated, murmuring frantically incessant complaints under your breath while banging dishes in the sink. Who wants to identify with the victim?

Widowhood turned out to be a blessing. A sense of humor—sharp, open—slowly emerged, shocking me with its spark. You started laughing. As when we contemplated the advisability of your trip to New York several years ago, soon after a previous brush with death—a blood clot that had migrated from an artery in your lower leg to your lungs. We were concerned about the applicability of your medical insurance. A "preexisting condition" such as pulmonary embolism could nullify it and slap me with huge, American-style medical bills. However, when I raised the possibility of anything going wrong *during* the flight, you replied lightheartedly, "That is the best-case scenario—no medical bills—they will just dump my body into the ocean and be done with it."

We often liked to amuse ourselves by laughing death in the face.

But when I recently asked you, "Are you afraid to die?"

You admitted a shy, "Yes."

I know that more than death, you are afraid of the accompanying pain. You have a jar of sleeping pills to help you through in case life becomes unbearable or just undignified, not up to your standards. You talk a lot about taking them when the time comes. You talk about it far too much for me to believe you would ever make use of them. I am happy that you have the comfort of that option in your mind, though. And the sadness of it all, even if artificially fueled and further fanned by your sense of drama, breaks my heart.

I don't want you to be alone when the time comes. But in all likelihood, alone you will be. I am away. I will stay away. Even in your most insane moments, you have never asked me to sacrifice my daughters, my pleasures, my freedom to take care of you instead. I will continue skiing. I will continue attending the opera—a passion I scorned you for when I was younger but nevertheless ended up absorbing. I will continue living my life away from you while the cancer devours you from within. Guilt? No, not really. I follow your baton. As I always have.

We each know. We each know the other knows. We each love. We each know how much the other loves. We each cry. But we cannot do it facing each other. We would each break.

Session 2
Kinderszenen

Transylvania, Near the Hungarian Border, Early 1960s

We are walking down the street, my little palm wrapped around your finger. It must be spring or summer, otherwise you would be pulling me in the red wooden sleigh across the deep snow. Szatmar, again under Romanian rule, is situated ten kilometers from the Hungarian border. Though both governments are marching to orders issued by the Kremlin, the heavy gates between the two countries are impenetrable, guarded by heavily armed soldiers.

We are going to visit my sister at school. Monika, fifteen, is in the Romanian Lyceum. She tears off a big portion of the sandwich she gets there for lunch and hands it to me. I extend my arm to grab it, my stomach growling in welcome, but feeling the injustice with a child's emotional radar, hesitate for a moment:

"Why is Monika giving me her lunch? Isn't she hungry?"

"No, she is not hungry today."

"I am not." Monika's eyes are following my mouth as I chew.

* *

I bathe in a little wooden tub you pull out from under the bed. You fill the tub with water that is heated in a big pot on the stove. The bed, where I always sleep in between you and my father, fills most of the one-room apartment. A huge floor-to-ceiling, blue-tiled chimney in one of the corners keeps us warm during the long, frozen winters. Your feet always bleed in winter—a reminder of the barefoot march at gunpoint across snowy Europe. Next to the chimney there's an armchair, which becomes a pullout sofa when Monika sleeps over. The rest of the time she goes to her dad's.

"Why does Monika say she goes to her dad? Daddy is right here."

You tell me that teenagers sometimes call school "dad." I am not convinced, but your underlying nervousness tells me not to probe any further.

I play on the thick rug and wet it with pee countless times to be only gently scolded. The *billi*, my little ceramic chamber pot, is stored underneath the bed. The toilet—the one the adults use during the day—is outside in the yard. It's a wooden structure with a hole on top. Some of our neighbors have sophisticated "English toilets" that flush.

You and my father fight, and he slams the door. I later reprimand him sternly for his bad behavior, and the tension is instantly released. He laughs, his big front teeth gap, the sacks under his eyes swell, then turn red. He wipes a tear and passes a finger along my cheek as if startled by its softness. At three years old, I am the only one able to tame him.

On weekends, we often go to the big park located in the heart of the city. It has a huge yellow, rainbow-like structure marking the entrance and a lake at the center. My father greets his friends, they chat, all are well-dressed, wearing gray or brown suits and neckties, sporting hats that they slightly lift or touch upon greeting. Some carry walking sticks, which frighten me a bit. I am introduced with all the respect due to a duchess.

On our way home from the park one day, struggling through the icy streets, I notice a giant figure all decked out in a red outfit and sporting a long white beard. It seems to have appeared out of nowhere and is standing motionless on the side of the road, surrounded by intoxicating-smelling bushes loaded with sparkling balls.

"What is *that*?" I am in awe.

"It's *Mikulas*," you reply. That's the Hungarian nickname for Saint Nicholas. My father often calls me *Mikulasom*, my Mikulas.

"Can we have one of these trees?" I implore. The shiny balls are what I am really after.

"No. We are Jewish," you attempt to reason with me. When you run out of explanations to my endless "whys," you give in and buy a tiny Christmas tree and a few glass decorations to go with it. Within five minutes from our arrival home, I wear you down into letting me hold one of the balls.

"Now look what you've done."

We both gaze at the shattered pieces that must have cost that day's wages, but your soft voice is devoid of anger.

From time to time, we visit the old Jewish cemetery. You light memorial candles and then sit by one of the graves, weeping. My father paces about, agitated.

"Who is buried here?" I ask, while hopping between and on the tombstones that seem to have been placed there for that purpose only.

"Your grandfather. Daddy's father."

"Then why is *Mommy* crying?" I insist.

"There is no place for me to cry for my own family, so I cry here," you reply.

That is puzzling.

"Don't they have their own graves?"

"No, they don't." You are irritated by now.

"Why not?"

"They just don't!"

There is a big, brown wardrobe along the wall facing the bed. My two friends Pityu (Peter) and Yoji (Joseph), who live in our building, make me pose in front of that piece of furniture as they spray scented water on me, mumble something, make a gesture across my face and chest, and place some red eggs in my hand. You are ill at ease at this Easter ritual being performed on your daughter, but with the war and the fear still fresh in your memory, let the ceremony proceed without showing your disapproval. You give them some *matzo*—flat unleavened bread we eat during Passover—in return.

I am among the youngest in nursery school. I look for my lunch bag amid the many scattered on the table in the corridor. My bag is light blue. Before I have a chance to get to it, a nasty little boy grabs it and refuses to hand it back.

"Give it to me. It's *my* bag." I stare straight at him.

"No! You are a filthy Jew," he says.

"No. *You* are a filthy Jew!" I reply, kicking my foot. I have no idea what it is that we are saying. An adult comes to my rescue, takes my bag away from the boy, and hands it to me.

My best friend is Mariana. We are playing by the hand-cranked water pump on the street corner, splashing water, getting wet. Later, we are in her family's warm kitchen where her mother, a checkered apron around her thick waist, serves us chicken soup.

"Eat your carrots. They help your eyesight," she says to me.

I don't like carrots and leave then anyway.

"And don't forget us when you go to your Palestina," she adds as if in an afterthought, a hint of jealousy even a three-and-a-half-year-old can't miss in her voice.

"What is she talking about?"

There's trouble at the *Unio*, the factory where my father works. I hear words I don't understand like "immigration certificate" and "fired." We soon take the train to the countryside and stay in a farmhouse. My parents work at a government fruit collection station. The local Gypsies bring berries picked in the forests high up in the mountains—you weigh the fruit and pay them, bread often being the currency of choice.

Two cows live on the farm and are milked every morning before spending their day out in the meadows. I stand by the milkmaid and get a sip of the steaming, creamy liquid straight from the red metal container she uses to collect it. It tastes like fresh grass and something else, warm and earthy.

There is a brook, a wooden bridge, and an occasional steam train passing by. Once, as I am playing in the clear water under the bridge, studying the tiny fish swimming to and fro, I realize it is late and my mom must be looking for me. In a hurry, I jump over the railway tracks just before the grill on the front of the black steam train chugs noisily past, missing me by a fraction of a second. I run to you, hide my face in your skirt, and pretend nothing happened.

We are back in the city. By now I am almost four years old. One day you ask me if I want to go to Palestina, explaining that it is a faraway land—a place where oranges grow. "Palestina." The word tastes like chocolate-filled wafers. I can imagine it on my tongue. As I ponder, you repeat your question as if it all depends on me. Already the little adventurer, I reply without hesitation, "Sure!"

Besides, like a little lamb, what else can I do but follow my mother wherever she goes? A few months later, I leave home for the first time.

The Voyage

Bucharest, Somewhere in the Mediterranean, Galilee

1964

People are crowded in the train station, saying their good-byes and sending off those who are heading "out." The Romanian government, as part of a political deal with the US, is allowing the Jewish population to emigrate. There is a one-time window of opportunity to flee the clutches of communism. Synagogues and street corners host heated debates. Where should we go? Your eldest sister chooses to pursue the legend of "Amerika," as it is known to us. Following a few months in transit—including an immigrants' camp in Rome—she finally settles in Brooklyn, New York, and never again leaves the boundaries of her adopted borough. The other, Erzsebet, is afraid to take on unknown explorations and stays put in her provincial, backward village. Agnes, one of my father's two surviving sisters, opts to remain in Bucharest (the other fled to Brazil during the war) and continues hiding her Jewish identity even from her own children. One of the first party members, she works as a journalist for the state-owned newspaper. The bosom of communism is comfortable for the faithful.

Most of the Jewish population, however, is on the move. Towns and villages are emptying the remainder of their surviving Jewish inhabitants. Household after household—all are packing. People leave behind their furniture, jewelry, cutlery, memories, and graves. We are allowed to take only the bare necessities with us. The containers are strictly searched by the authorities, and anyone defying the rules is condemned to long prison terms. Few take the risk. No one complains. There is no time to reflect or hesitate. We are in a rush to leave before the wind changes course.

The nightly train ride thrills me, with some young people sharing our carriage, smoking and playing cards way past my bedtime, offering me chewing gum (a novelty) by way of consolation. The miracle of an elevator at my aunt Agnes's immense apartment building—we stand in it, and the doors suddenly open onto a different floor! My beloved doll, initially not included in our luggage—apparently some people had tried to smuggle out jewelry inside dolls—finally ends up being packed in one of our two big wooden cases. Despite my tears, the fake diamond necklace I want to wear is nonnegotiable and taken off almost forcibly. It could be mistaken for the real thing. In Ceausescu's Romania, fear is life's main ingredient.

It is 1964.

We climb the stairs onto the plane for what would be my first flight.

"You would *live* in an airport," you commented, many years later, referring to my endless travel.

We embark on a magical trip that leads us through a castle on the outskirts of Vienna—rented by the Jewish Agency to house immigrants on their way to Israel—a night train ride where the passengers excitedly point out the lights of Venice flickering on the distant horizon, and finally, a bus ride through the length of Italy that stops in Bari. Waiting in line to board our next form of transportation, its dark silhouette floating on the black waters beyond the pier, my screams pierce the Puglian sky and assault nerves already on edge. I refuse to set foot onboard. What I can't put into words is my terror of falling into the cold wetness. I've never seen a ship before and—only a child would know why—I imagine its floors to be full of holes. All worries evaporate when I am bribed finally with a chocolate bar to take the risk and find myself running up and down the full length of the vessel, a vast playground. During the sea journey, in between being seasick and worrying about me tripping off the deck, you still manage to flirt coquettishly with every young crewman.

The ship calls at ports in Greece and Cyprus, but eager to start their new lives, nobody is interested in tourism. One heard a rumor that they, the "Israelis," are in need of locksmiths to build the young country. Another believes presenting oneself as a tailor is even better. The camps these leftover European Jews barely survived taught them the importance of made-up professional histories; faking the right one could make the difference between life and death. They reinvent themselves anew to be "useful" yet again. At dawn, a gray outline appears on the horizon: Haifa.

Our new homeland welcomes us with the same hectic nonchalance it offers all its fatigued newcomers—with blazing sun and a thick layer of dust. The very same evening, we are hurriedly deposited by our taxi driver, together with our two suitcases—the two big trunks containing the heavy goose-feather eiderdowns would arrive later—in front of a small wooden hut in a godforsaken village in the north of the country. The driver gives us the keys and, as it is late Friday afternoon with the Sabbath about to lend its holy grace to our universe, vanishes without a trace. With him go our former lives.

You promptly sit on one of the suitcases and start crying, refusing to even enter this sorry excuse for a cabin. You did not survive Auschwitz for *this*, to be living in barracks again. It takes my father, better accustomed to Budapest than to lost villages in the Galilee, exactly two weeks to make a decision. We leave the village, the iron-framed beds and straw mattresses offered by the government, and board the next bus in the general direction of Tel Aviv, none of us quite sure at which stop to get off.

On one of my visits to see you—I was living in New York and you were still relatively well (I guess going forward, we will refer to "before" and "after" the cancer)—I suggested that we travel a bit to the north. Above Nazareth, on the winding roads of the Galilee, I noticed signs displaying the name of the village we were taken to on that Friday before dusk. Giv'at ha-More. Even the signs looked hopeless, the paint peeling off as if no one had bothered with them since they had been planted there. The small, one-family houses with the barren dirt yards in between and the two-story apartment buildings were still filled with hordes of children, no one to wipe their runny noses, chasing each other on the unpaved ground. Elderly men sat in front of the houses on folding chairs, their toothless jaws endlessly chewing some invisible tobacco, gazing with foggy eyes into thin air. But "thin air" is not a good choice of words, because everything was covered in a thick, yellow dust of neglect. The only visible change from the time we had inhabited these buildings was the color of their occupants, the place obviously being a "dumping ground" for each new wave of immigrants, the latest being from Ethiopia.

While you debated, the bus passed Petah Tikva and was approaching Tel Aviv. We randomly got off in Bnei Braq. My father may have had an acquaintance who had mentioned the name, so it sounded familiar. Some Hungarian-speaking strangers took us in for a few days. You found a job making prayer shawls, *tallith*, sewing on the collars, embroidered with gold or silver thread, adding stitched verses from the holy scriptures onto the four corners of the cloth, and tying the frills. Paid by the number of articles completed, you were obviously annoyed with my constant appeals for you to let me tie the frills with my tiny fingers, having to waste precious time to untie and redo them. Those religious relics were my only toys, as I examined and reexamined each of the woven details during the long hours I sat at your feet watching you labor. We delivered the finished items loaded on my baby carriage, only to be replaced by another stack while arguing. I quickly got tired and refused to walk farther, and you gave in finally and pushed the heavy cargo with me on top, sweating in the sweltering heat to which you were unaccustomed.

A year later, instead of going home after kindergarten, I used to head to one of the apartments you were hired to clean—to find you kneeling on all fours, wiping the floor with a wet rag.

But by the time I turned eight, my father's workshop was well established, and you were back to being a proper housewife. You had signed a contract, applied for a mortgage, and on Saturday afternoons we used to visit the construction site where raw concrete columns and rusting metal snakes were emerging from the dry soil. A few months later, my father was polishing the stony floors with a mechanical chisel, one inch at a time, sweat soaking his white undershirt and dripping off his brow, until they shined to your satisfaction. Part of the balcony was walled in and fitted with a door to create a semi-room for me, and we moved into my first permanent home and your last one.

Session 4

The Queen of Kitsch

Suburbs of Tel Aviv

I hate your collections. The endless bouquets of artificial flowers, the crystal vases, the porcelain figurines, the cheap pictures covering every inch of the walls, the carpets gathered from who knows where. One can walk barefoot anywhere in your apartment without ever stepping off those rugs.

Your apartment—you think the whole world envies you for it—is a temple to cheap, worthless kitsch absurdly situated in the heart of Bnei Braq, the ugliest, most religious neighborhood in Israel, the navel of the renunciation of beauty on earth. It is located like a sore—glitzy, literally *shining* thorns; see the silver wallpaper in the bathroom—in the heart of filth and poverty, spitting in the face of its surroundings. A tribute to Marilyn Monroe, a poster of her in fishnet stockings, strikes a suggestive pose by your bed. A shrine to nudity and earthly pleasures. You constructed a place of worship to pagan aesthetics in the middle of a sea of pious fanatics praying for their sinful souls and looking for heavenly rewards.

Even now, facing a clear and imminent death sentence, you denounce their God. Any God.

I resent but admire your genius. You are imitating Elvis Presley and Andy Warhol without ever having heard their names; shining red 1960s pop art table and chairs constitute your "dining room"; you sew clothes that your nineteen-year-old granddaughter wants to pinch from you. To my surprise, I occasionally happen to find similar designs in the trendiest stores in Paris. I am humbled to admit that, while only a couple of years ago I reprimanded you for buying some silver shoes—how could a grown woman walk around in such a ridiculous color?—I recently ended up paying a hefty sum for an almost identical pair on rue du Temple in the heart of the Parisian fashion world. You become enraged when I tell you I won't be seen with you in those see-through, flimsy skirts and low-cut—*very* low-cut—shirts you put on for an elegant dinner out. At your advanced age, you are more avant-garde than most twenty-year-olds in the East Village. Where is the border between art and lunacy? Somewhere in your head.

"After my death, don't sell the apartment!" you recently ordered. You want me to keep that psychedelic place as a shrine to you, a monument and museum. In your conceited mind, you truly believe that I will. I would rather blow it up. To rid myself of the memories of all the pain that is still steeped into those cheap Sheetrock walls, the violent fights between you and my father that served as background music to my childhood. Your recurrent motif: "Why didn't Hitler finish with me right there and then instead of condemning me to live in this hell?"

And, after the lightning and thunder were over, after the armchairs were placed back on their feet and the broken plates cleared away, you would stand by the kitchen sink, banging dishes, mumbling to yourself for hours, keeping up a maddening monotonous chanting of grievances. I would listen to you and pray to God to take my father to Him and put an end to the torture. Take my father, of course. Never you. You were the victim. You had perfected that role to a form of art.

I don't blame you. As the third, unwanted girl—another useless mouth to feed—you were, obviously, not taken to finger-painting classes to develop your budding artistic talents. I doubt anyone appreciated your attempts at creating beauty. All you got was a sharp slap on the cheek and a nasty remark from one of your older sisters, calling you "lazy" for neglecting the more immediate household chores. So the art world lost one of its promising talents, and it all mutated into artificial roses and shiny dresses.

I recently joined an organized tour of an annex to the Musée des Arts Decoratifs, the former private home of the de Camondo family, housing the most impressive surviving collection of eighteenth-century art in Paris. His son and heir having been killed as a pilot in WWI, Moise, the family patriarch, donated the house to the French State. Neither the heroic self-sacrifice of the son nor the generous donation of the father prevented their beloved country from actively assisting in the deportation of Moise's daughter, Beatrice, and his grandchildren, a few years later. All were murdered in Auschwitz. Beatrice is believed to have survived until two weeks prior to the liberation of the camp.

Wide-eyed, we walked through the magnificent rooms, the priceless furniture, chandeliers, and polished mirrors almost as impressive as those in Versailles. We reached the elegant dining room, still fitted out with hand-painted plates, crystal wine glasses, and silverware as if the dinner guests were just about to arrive. And I tried to imagine the woman who grew up calling that palace home, wearing striped rags with a rusty spoon as her most prized possession. The chattels, unlike their owners, were hidden away during the war and emerged—"luckily," commented our eloquent guide—intact. I looked at the "lucky" furniture, the pictures, the antique rugs, the tapestries—and wondered about their true value. One of the reception room furniture sets had been bought by Moise de Camondo for over a million gold coins. I am sure his daughter would have gladly bartered it all for one loaf of bread, perhaps even a single slice, just a few years later. It was a tough exchange rate in Auschwitz, a crude validation of rudimentary economic principles. When it really came down to it, those precious possessions were worthless, useless. While the group marveled at all that beauty, I saw only *things*. Meaningless objects. Their only substantive value derived from the sophisticated mind cultivated to appreciate and take pleasure in them, the descanting eyes trained to caress them, the exquisite taste and persistence that adoringly put them together, and the generous heart that shared them. These items and the concepts they represented were as dead as their former owners.

As I walked down the stairs leading to the metro, still under the impression of the collection and the tragedy it personified, it dawned on me that I never really understood you. That in your own way—in what I foolishly perceived to be your insanity—you were a collector of beauty just like the old de Camondo patriarch was. He would have, no doubt, turned in his grave at the ridiculous comparison of your kitschy, cheap, hideous, artificial junk crowding an apartment located at the end of a Bnei-Braqi dirt road to his Parisian marvel situated on the edge of Park Monceau and toured by visitors from all over the world. But what you lacked in educated palate and means, you made up for in your desperate quest for splendor. I have done you injustice. Wronged you. I was blind to the fact that you could, indeed, be twin souls with this man who willed not to move the tiniest item of his collection from its designated spot. That during your lonely, sleepless, nightly tours surveying your domain of two tiny, crumbling rooms, you were the *comtesse* of your mansion, none less grand than any museum in the city of Paris. And you loved it with the same passion. You were right. And I, in my narrow and pedestrian interpretation, in my scorn for your imagination, was too obtuse to appreciate your genius of turning dust into gold. The gift that made you as rich as the de Camondos and beyond. That you, who came back from the very same cemetery our humble family ended up sharing with this grand, fabulous one—all on the same plain of smoke and ashes—had longed for and succeeded in possessing, owning, holding something beyond that rusty, crooked spoon you were allotted.

You never cease to amaze me. In your mideighties, you are a huge financial as well as emotional drain on me. A demanding and selfish, vain old woman, manipulative, suffering from a whole encyclopedia of mental disorders. Your unrestrained narcissism, for example. Hardly ever do we eat in a restaurant without you leaning closer and whispering to me, "That man sitting at the table behind you does not take his eyes off me."

I discreetly turn around to see a handsome man, about my age, chatting enthusiastically with his young and attractive lady companion.

"That man is engrossed in conversation with the woman he is with and wouldn't notice even me. And I am much closer to his age," I absent-mindedly mouth back.

"He would not notice *you* but keeps looking at *me*," you conclude in a triumphant voice.

I watch your capacity for self-delusion—persuading yourself that your beauty hasn't and will never fade—and I salute you.

You mold the truth to your needs; you accuse and viciously attack me. You make me pay for everything I supposedly got from you in the past and for the meager inheritance you may or may not leave me in the future. You are a true witch and a monster.

In one of those moods that you are so prone to, I hear your voice over the phone, shrilled with malice: "You are competing with your sister in neglecting me."

I hang up. You are an expert in hitting the target—straight through the heart. I am hurt over and over again, no matter how predictable these transformations are. And yet, within no more than a few days, perhaps a week, I end up dialing your number again. I cannot bring myself to abandon you.

Is this "love"?

I fear your madness. I fear it the way one fears an enemy that lies within.

Tali, a childhood friend, accompanied me recently on one of my shopping sprees. She watched as I piled on the checkout counter a mountain of items, topping it all with an artistic shoe sculpture I found irresistible. A daily visitor to your apartment—as adolescents we used to gossip into the wee hours of the night—Tali could not stop herself from observing: "Do you notice you are just like your mother? Give it a few years, and your apartment will look exactly like hers."

I stop on my heels. I shiver. I then swipe my credit card in the machine.

Why do I still need you? I need you to be the barrier between my own madness and me.

Session 5

Home

Suburbs of Tel Aviv, 1967

I hesitated for barely a moment before abandoning my tricycle in the middle of the street and, familiar with the procedure, ran directly to the shelter situated in the basement of the next-door building. Even as a six-year-old, I understood that the risk of my red bike being stolen was worth taking in order to rapidly reach the safety of the bunker.

As I ran down the stairs and entered the dark, cement-walled room, three dozen or so tired eyes looked up at me. The old were leaning on the walls in silent resignation—some praying, only their lips moving in a quiet murmur—while the young mothers were trying to pacify screaming babies. With neighboring countries' radio stations already calling the war a victory and promising slaughter on the streets of Tel Aviv, everyone's nerves were frazzled; the crying did not help the already strained atmosphere. I was looking for, but couldn't find you. As I turned around to go back to our apartment, you materialized; breathless, scolding me in a hushed voice: "I was searching everywhere for you!"

"Couldn't you figure out I would be smart enough to come directly to the bunker?" I was preparing to argue, but the wailing siren silenced my budding protests.

We both settled in a corner of the basement, waiting either for bombs to fall or the signal to let us free. We weren't expecting my father to join us. At fifty-two, he was still the fearless man of his youth, lighting one cigarette with the butt of another while listening to radio reports from the front. He was not running anywhere. My childish efforts at scolding him fell upon, literally, deaf ears. My father's hearing had been severely impaired, a "souvenir" from a bullet passing right next to his left ear while wrestling away from a Hungarian fascist execution squad on the banks of the Danube. He had known worse.

The mounting and descending wail of the siren released us from our confinement. Relieved to find the tricycle in the same place I had left it, I headed home and asked to have some of the chocolate that was stashed away in the closet. Weeks before, as soon as rumors about an imminent war started to spread, dreading a long siege, people had stocked up on food and supplies. Being new immigrants, you had no financial reserves to lean on and couldn't buy much. But with a war you had survived by the skin of your teeth still fresh in your memory, the voices of your little brothers begging for another slice of bread still ringing in your ears, one item was secured regardless of any financial constraints: chocolate. There was a tall pile consisting of two blue packs of my favorite, thick chocolate bars—you couldn't afford more than two of those—and about ten smaller red bars with the familiar picture of a yellow cow on the package. My repeated requests to have some were met with a shocking, odd refusal; it was reserved for emergency, in case the war turned out badly. I guess your earlier fear of having lost me was still vivid enough for you to relent and let me have just a few squares on this occasion.

Having lost most of your loved ones twenty-three years before, and escaping the communist regime just three years earlier with nothing but the clothes on your backs, you were now facing another survival test—helpless, this time with a child a month shy of her seventh birthday in tow. How was it possible to retain your sanity? There was talk of leaving for Canada. Or, more vaguely, to America. But those were pointless dreams. In reality, you had neither the means nor the inclination to pack and wander again into the unknown.

Unlike your prior encounters with fate, this time it had a miracle in store: the war ended in victory.

On Yom Kippur 1973, I was old enough to form memories. Again, sirens. Blowing so unexpectedly on the holiest of days. Cars suddenly speeding along roads normally deserted to secular bike riders and pedestrian synagogue goers. Confusion. Should we turn on the radio? Descend to the bunker? Was it just another military exercise? No longer a "victim" by definition, you were able to send me off to bravely participate in the war effort; I volunteered to replace the postman, a reservist called in to active duty.

The "Gulf War" was not even an actual war—but how else can one define missiles being targeted at and landing on a civilian population, women and children sitting behind paper-plastered windows in sealed rooms with gas masks covering their faces, babies in gas-resistant cradles, all waiting for the explosion?

How many people on the face of this earth can attest to being subjected to the menace of being gassed to death not once, but twice in the same lifetime?

You won that dubious honor. An old woman, alone, trying to figure out how to put on the mask, practically choking in it from a sudden nosebleed. The alerts on Israeli television were announced in many languages, but Hungarian wasn't one of them. You were at a loss. When you could no longer rely on the kindness of neighbors to take you in to wait out the attacks, when Monika refused to have you at her place, we developed a rather complicated procedure—but it worked. In my New York apartment, I would continuously have CNN on, listening to the reports, getting real-time information. As soon as a bombardment commenced, I would quickly call to instruct you to put on the gas mask. We would stay on the phone together until the reporter announced that the missile had landed on some other unfortunate place. I would then liberate you from the "sealed room" and the mask. I was hoping that being on the other end of the line would help relieve some of your loneliness, even though my presence was only virtual. When one of those missiles fell only a block away from your apartment building, when you were too exhausted and stressed to even attempt putting on the mask, my then husband and I decided that the torture had gone far enough and sent you a plane ticket to the safety of the Big Apple. Where, two days after landing, you told me that even the threat of missiles was easier to bear than sharing the same living quarters with me. But that was to be expected. In fact, it reassured me that you had swiftly recovered from the trauma and were back in shape.

You still spoke practically no Hebrew, could not read a street sign or the menu at a restaurant, but you came to prefer a pita with hummus and oriental spiced meats to goulash. Threats of an additional war received barely a shrug. You missed polite European manners but would not give up on living among the Israeli riffraff for all the gallantry of France and Italy put together. You were finally at home.

Session 6

Stories My Father Never Wrote

Suburbs of Tel Aviv, 1968

I see his lips each time I look in the mirror. I remember him laughing. I can still sense his manly smell of cigarettes and his warm, dry kisses which I much preferred to your slimy, wet ones. I was six years old; we had just arrived in Israel a couple years before. We moved from one rented apartment to the next like Gypsies, carrying our few belongings in a fully loaded baby carriage. You and I slept on the one bed while my father slept inside the big drawer that served to store the bedding during the day. I would then settle next to him and beg for a story. And then another.

"Just one more, Daddy, *please!*"

"No, *mokus kirai* (king of the squirrels). It's time for you to sleep."

I would plead, and he would finally relent on condition that I stay beside him in the low, makeshift bed. He would make up endless stories on the spot.

"Had I put these stories down in writing and published them, I'd be a well-known author," he would fantasize from time to time.

But he never did; there were more urgent tasks, such as making a living, to pursue.

A man who had finally sired a child—he wanted a boy but fell in love with the girl—in middle age. The former *bon vivant*, indulging in women, liquor, and gambling, had finally fallen into the net of a red-faced baby. His pride in me was as thick as a physical element. Even as a young babe, I could feel it enveloping me in its adoring protection. Unlike you, he did not ask for anything in return. Just the right, sometimes, ever so gently, to run his finger—rendered coarse and callused in the course of years of hard manual labor—down my round cheek, savoring its softness. When I touch my daughters' smooth, peachy faces, amazed at their velvety texture, we— my father and I—are one.

We spent months investigating the spiral routes of planets, memorizing the precise distance of each from the sun. He introduced me to Jules Verne and Rabindranath Tagore. He paid careful attention to my explanations about a secret code I invented and studied my rudimentary submarine designs— interior *and* exterior—as if they were made by a renowned engineer. He sat in my tiny room searching for a meaning in my favorite Salvador Dalí posters and strained his half-deaf ears to listen to Pink Floyd. No one could have more faithfully, for hours on end, waited for me at the bus stop to come home from my entertainments in order to protect me from the gangs of shady types that lurked around the dark corners. He was my avid admirer and best buddy.

He never did anything that could have been construed as abusive, but my father's inherent sexuality was so overpowering that by the age of thirteen, I started feeling uncomfortable around him. I was walking a bit bent to hide my budding breasts, suppressing my womanhood, silently angry when he once, only once, bent over behind me while I was reading and kissed me fleetingly on my lips.

At eighteen, as soon as I got my driver's license, I started, like all adolescents, nagging him to buy me a car. Even the price of a used one was steep in Israel thirty-five years ago. He tried but could not resist the temptation of pleasing his daughter, seeing the glow in her eyes, having her wrap her arms around his neck and kiss him, proclaiming, "You are the best daddy in the world!"

He recognized the slightly off note—the affection showered on him being a product of true love but also a bit faux, with just a hint of manipulation—but didn't mind it at all. And when he came to visit me in Jerusalem for my twenty-second birthday, and I asked to go to the most exclusive restaurant, far exceeding his price range, he didn't say no; he just sat there while I ate, pretending not to be hungry, and later grabbed a quick sandwich at a cheap stand. My stomach still turns at the recollection of my juvenile selfishness.

There was a price to pay.

I knew he wanted me to be Daddy's little girl. To always remain Daddy's little girl.

"I like to see you laughing," was his wish and my command.

So, already a student, I still talked to him and giggled like a little girl, using that falsetto, cheerful voice, always pretending to be happy for my daddy. That was the bargain we struck.

Until I grew up. Couldn't help becoming a woman.

But all that happened later.

There were three on our tiny island. We were a triangle. My opinions were respected even before I could complete full sentences. My "pearls of wisdom" were recited to friends over the weekly card games. I was smarter. I was more sophisticated. I was groomed to be the crown jewel. The princess who would eventually be ashamed of the parents who had raised her to the throne. And would shake them off as discarded dust.

"Jaguar is the best car in the world," said the man who never had a driver's license.

I drove a light-blue Jaguar "S" type.

"The Plaza Athénée is the best hotel in the world," said the man who never set foot in Paris.

I drank dozens of twenty-six-euro cocktails at the flashy lobby on 25 Avenue Montaigne.

For his sake, I lived the big dreams he planted in me. At the end, they were not that difficult to fulfill. But it was too late. And all I am left with is the taste of regret in my mouth.

Session 7

Rashomon

Though a bit on the periphery, making only occasional appearances, there actually was one other persona in our secluded universe: Monika. Your first husband and my father were business partners "back there." Until the scandalous affair was followed by divorce. Remarriage to your Don Juan of a lover was your only way to regain respectability after being depicted as the town whore. My father left his old wife—forgetting her devotion to him and how she had saved his life during the war—to move in with you, carrying with him, according to the family legend, nothing but two shirts. Monika, my half sister and the only reminder of what everyone wanted to forget, moved between the two split families like an uninvited guest.

Those were lonely years.

I used to wait for the bus Monika was supposed to arrive on at the stop near our rented apartment, wherever it happened to be at the time. She attended nursing school in Jerusalem; her visits were sporadic and, in those pre-telephone-in-every-household days, unannounced. On Friday afternoons, I would often be standing at the station, knowing that the Sabbath would soon fall upon us. I stood patiently as one bus followed another—it was the number 61—each disgorging its unfamiliar passengers, each empty of her. Stubborn, I kept waiting, ignoring your gentle persuasions calling me in, telling me it was too late, that she was not coming that weekend, waiting until the darkness and the cold forced me home.

She made it to my first day of school, though. I was accompanied by all three—my dad, Monika, and you—but only she could share in that experience and be "useful" in my new environment. She volunteered to assist the teacher while taking note of the items we needed to prepare for the following day—a wrapped notebook, a page filled with multiple copies of the letter "H" written as neatly as our unsteady hands could manage, and a pencil. Without her, I wouldn't have known any of that. My language skills thus far could be summed up in the only sentence that, having rehearsed it endless times in my head, I managed to say in my whole year in kindergarten:

"Shoshana, I'd like to play with the ball."

Twelve years my senior, Monika was more of an aunt to me than a sister, but I didn't realize it then—she was the only one I had. For her, I must have been the annoying, much younger, spoilt little brat who hit her butt as she swirled, dancing tango in the living room with one of my father's remote relatives who, after the war, popped up out of nowhere in Uruguay.

Together, they were charged with babysitting me when my parents, on a rare outing, went to watch a movie. At seventeen, she must have tried to act very grown up-ish, a performance rendered futile by someone banging on her behind.

But there were tender moments, such as when she took me to Tel Aviv for my first haircut. Up until then I'd had long blondish-red hair you admired and persistently curled each night around strings of cloth so that I would wake up in the morning with nice ringlets. You then tied those up in a white or, alternatively, pink ribbon you ironed and starched to perfection. One can only imagine the reaction that Austro-Hungarian hairdo received from the Israeli *sabras*, the prickly little natives who had grown up in the sweltering heat of the Israeli sand dunes. Monika, being the first bridge between our European indoors and the "barbarian" outside environment, was determined to save me from further humiliation. One morning, in your absence, she took me to Tel Aviv, sat me on the chair at a hair salon, and asked the stylist—actually a barber—for a short, contemporary haircut. When you first saw a familiar, boyish-looking child excitedly running toward you, all smiles and affection, you burst into tears.

We went sometimes to the park together, Monika and I: She, a miniature, coquettish brunette with a perfect figure, tight skirt, and heels. I, all white skin and freckles, gap-toothed, was dressed in one of your creations—a frilly baby-blue dress no Israeli kid would be seen dead in, with white socks and black patent leather shoes. She read and scouted the place for admiring young men while I, who would later grow to be a giant in comparison, was left to my business in the sand box or on the swings. Monika was the most delicate Japanese porcelain doll to my robust, red-haired ball of energy. Her exquisite, oddly Asian features, long black hair, tiny but perfectly proportioned body, and shapely legs were a few years ahead of contemporary fashion, and her petite breasts, the kind much admired in the subsequent Twiggy years, were at the time a constant source of embarrassment to her. That identical look would be much in vogue years later, when her traits would capriciously materialize in my daughter, her niece.

The ever-turbulent relationship between Monika and you, the womb we both shared, seemed, at least initially, not to have a real impact on our own alliance. Being your spitting image, I could somehow tolerate and, quite often, comprehend your insanity, your vanity, the see-through shirts and bright colors you wore. They did not please me, but neither did they embarrass me as much. Truth be told, nowadays I often find myself donning similarly extravagant outfits. Yet Monika had a lower level of tolerance. Your excesses left her aghast.

Or was it the "original sin" of the divorce that created a wound that could never heal? You each had different versions of that unfinished past.

"I knocked and knocked—Mom was inside the house with your father, and they wouldn't open the door."

My middle-aged sister, normally reserved to the point of being a tad cold, had tears in her eyes as she recalled the shocking event experienced by her twelve-year-old self. The trauma clearly fresh in her mind, she took a sip from the cup of coffee clenched between her fingers in an attempt to recompose herself. And I imagined the budding teenager, shy and introverted, just back from school, shut out of her home, betrayed by a mother locked in the embrace of a stranger, her so-far sheltered life shattered by the subsequent divorce.

I could relate to the pain, but only as an outsider. And I was utterly unequipped to comprehend the hatred it produced. Nor could I relate to your ocean-deep corresponding guilt—guilt that produced vicious circles of silent blame issued by Monika, and furtive, wordless, perpetual, apologetic defenses mounted faintly by you. Outbursts of misnamed, misdirected fights over irrelevant issues-turned-excuses veiling bottomless wells of historic rancor. And, as usual, phones being slammed down on both ends.

In this version of the classic Japanese film *Rashomon*, not only the variations of the story differ, but, to complicate matters, so do the roles. In Kurosawa's movie, the wife is always the wife, the bandit the bandit, the priest the priest, and so on—even as they tell alternate narratives. In our drama, however, the story changes.

"She is lying! I never left her outside," you proclaim vehemently when I once made the error of recounting Monika's accusation to you.

The villain and the victim perform an ever-shifting dance. Both of you are virtuosos of self-pity and righteousness, and my head is spinning, trying to follow the whirlwind of tears, blame, and counterclaims flying to and fro from reddening eyes.

One minute, my heart goes out to protect you from Monika's groundless charges, and the next I pity the homeless child she became as a result of your selfish, foolish actions. And then, in yet another twist, you are blaming yourself and defending *her*— this weak and rejected child of yours who never had a warm place to call home—and you now wish to correct past wrongs. In what seems a sudden and unjust turn against the unsuspecting bystander I thus far considered myself to be, you advocate Monika's case, and presently I am the one who merits no sympathy—after all, the robust and most resilient pup in the litter is, naturally, expected to pull the bulk of the weight.

"Hey, why is that?" I protest. "What makes me so privileged, so undeserving in your eyes?"

I plead my case—in vain. You both manipulate each other with minor success and me with far more impressive results. I am crushed between your respective weeping and grievances. I figure you gave birth to me, so I need to be loyal to you and seldom see my sister. But in your court, guilt is a permanent resident: you keep questioning me about our estrangement, slyly hinting that I may have brought it about.

The outbursts between the two of you, the slammed phones and mutual accusations, become more violent and frequent. I have to maneuver between the two of you as if performing an intricate ballet, each single miscalculated step possibly leading to a mine field and a chain of explosions.

Eventually, instead of choosing sides, I tried to stay away from you all. My visits to Israel were few and far between. And on one of those rare occasions, in the old market in Lod—a poor half-Arab, half-Jewish slum known for nothing but its proximity to the airport—the complete rupture that swept Monika and me apart finally occurred.

She had suggested that we have lunch together at a hidden secret of a restaurant, a tumbling hut in a narrow alley on the outskirts of the market. They have legendary hummus, and their shish kabob is sought after by connoisseurs of such fare. As her husband dropped us off, we passed stalls of pungent olives, feathered chickens running around, and mountains of oriental spices. When we finally reached our destination, as befitted an establishment of this type, we were told that there had been a power outage and no cooking could be done until further notice. We had to make do with the hummus and pickles that were unceremoniously laid before us, which were splendid.

And then she told me she had reached the point of no return. She could no longer tolerate your presence in her life. She wanted nothing from you and would do nothing for you, even asked me to never mention your name again. For her, you were already dead and buried.

"Even if Mom were to die this very instant, I wouldn't want to know nor would I care," she declared.

And she was true to her word.

I am neither God nor judge, no authority on right and wrong. To a large extent, I understood. I did not hold against

Monika the long nights I sat up worrying about you not picking up the phone, wondering whether you were lying in agony on the floor trying to reach it after falling and breaking a hip or if your phone was simply out of order. I could not just call my sister, living barely thirty minutes away, and ask her to hop over and check. It was hard, but I did understand. I had been too close to cutting off all relationship with you to blame my sister for doing just that. But I have not seen Monika since. I didn't make the effort. Neither did she. And when you asked about her, when you kept wondering why she cut you off so coldly, I never told you about that last meeting. I couldn't bring myself to. I just shrug my shoulders and let you keep missing her.

Being a mother myself, I now realize how easy it is to vilify a mother, to turn her into a scapegoat for all our shortcomings and failures. A mother is a straightforward target. She almost volunteers to stand there, to willingly take the blame. How can a child resist the temptation? But it is *too* easy. I refuse to take the cheap route of judging you. When I was younger, the risk of arrogant ignorance was too high. As time passes, the risk of someday finding myself in the defendant's seat is absolute. Just a matter of time. Am I, therefore, trying to pre-vindicate myself from future harsh hearings conducted by my own offspring? Probably. Even if I already know that, like any judgment handed out by the young, it will be predetermined and cruel.

I haven't seen my beautiful sister for years, and perhaps

in the interim she has re-blossomed to be the flower she once was. I want to pick up the phone and call her. But what can I say when the real link between us—our slowly dying mother—is taboo? I let the moment pass.

Monika is now sixty-two. The reddish ringlets in my hair are still there but now manufactured by L'Oréal and covering advancing gray patches. Was the meeting in that dusty market restaurant our last? Are we to spend whatever is left of our lives as strangers? Not because of us, but as an indirect yet very direct result of *your* long arm, your influence over my life, your eternal weight that all else is measured by? Will there be forgiveness in our future, or is my relationship with my sister another victim of your martyrdom?

I do not blame you. We are all pawns in the gray shadows of life, where there is no "right" or "wrong." There is only pain. And love is not enough to make it all better.

Monika and I will live the rest of our lives with very different mothers etched into our memories and a great disparity between the narratives woven into our stories. The mother is sometimes the child; the older sister turns out to be the smaller and more fragile; the mean witch chokes on her own spite; the narrator is an interested party tooting her own horn until suddenly pulled into the fray; the role of the "sufferer" is coveted and eyed by each actor in turn—in a circus of acrobatically astonishing emotional manipulation. And each of these versions and roles is as true as any of the others.

One mother, two daughters, and the endless possibilities of hurt.

Which leaves just the two of us for this last tango. You, always a brilliant dancer, are the leader, and I stumble clumsily along. Just the two of us dancing in the confines of your overcrowded, overdecorated apartment, between the pictures, statues, porcelain figurines, crystal vases, artificial flowers gathering dust, leather armchairs, macramé napkins. Dancing under dangerously low-hanging chandeliers. We twirl along transatlantic phone lines, tangled in a desperate embrace. Monika has retired from the ball and left me the only recipient of your unique potion—a mixture of venom, seduction, and love. Which I grudgingly yet willingly suck.

Part II

DEPARTURES

December 14

The suitcase open on the floor accommodates in its belly the latest shopping list you dictated to me over the phone: foie gras, chocolate bonbons filled with liqueur, and both sweetened and unsweetened chestnut puree. I will buy the raspberries, your favorite, on my way to the airport and pack them in my carry-on luggage so they arrive at their destination as fresh as possible. Which, if any, of these will you be able to taste? Regardless, I dutifully buy the best quality and add a few additional products. Who could resist her mother's dying wish? When was I ever able to resist any of your wishes? Or, rather, commands. I marched to your drum day in and day out with the illusion of absolute freedom—as far away from you as could be, all the way to Japan, the US, Europe—and all the while I was but a puppet to your needs, desires, plans.

Our last voyage together. At least, I hope it is. Because I cannot take these emotional ups and downs any longer. I cannot take the threat of your imminent death hanging over my head for the past four years, looming over my life, each *mini-crisis wringing me out like a cloth drenched in its own tears. There's got to be an end to this soap opera or it becomes a farce too ridiculous to bear. You must die.*

But the journey I look forward to. Like the one we took so many years ago, sailing across the sea: only now the roles are reversed. I am no longer a helpless little girl, and you are no longer the guiding goddess. I imagine it to be as if I were Papageno, holding your hand, protecting and helping my Papagena to cross the river of fire. We are bound to silence. Well, that one requires some imagination, given your endless nonsensical chatter. But let's continue. We cross the bridge between life and death. Your hand in mine, you draw on my strength; I make this voyage with you, for you. Fear not. I am strong enough for the two of us, and you can lean on me and trust my grip. Let me lead you, step by step. Nothing bad can happen if I am the one escorting you, even if I am ushering you to your death.

You gave me the gift of life. I give you the gift of death. Mine is the more precious—a rarity. With this one act of mercy, I pay you back for all those years you cared for me since I took my first breath on this earth. In fact, this is the purpose of my existence. To be here for you now.

Courage, Mama. I will take care of everything. Do not look down into the abyss, just follow my footstep; this time the marionette is leading the puppeteer. Trust me and let me be your hero and savior. With your full accord and awareness, I will lead you to your death.

There is, alas, no choir, no audience watching the parade, no nail-biting crowds, no friend, no neighbor. Just the intimacy of the two of us as we were when you cradled me in your womb. Reversed. I wrap what is left of your ragged doll of a body in my arms, careful not to hurt; now, birth is replaced by death.

I brace myself. I close the suitcase. Mommy. Wait for me. I am on my way.

Session 8

Was It Love?

Tokyo, 1987

I ran away from you.
All the way to the other end of the world.

How can one recall a marriage without the influence of hindsight, of the eventual divorce? How can one faithfully reconstruct those early days of optimism when we were both young and innocent, believing to be in love?

First, there was the karaoke bar in Roppongi. I had left my father to his slow death, but for all practical purposes, I was already an orphan. He was no longer able to protect me. Attending to whatever was left of the husband you hated, abandoned to the thankless job of caring for and finally burying him, you were drowning under the burden, unable to care for me. With nothing to my name but a few bar-exam review books, I had been living out of a suitcase for months. After landing in Tokyo, fulfilling a lifelong dream of travel in the "exotic Far East," I settled at a *gaijin* house (an "alien house," a sort of a youth hostel) where lots of unfriendly "foreigners" (Caucasians) shared rooms costing approximately ten dollars per night, all working at nightclubs to make money for further Asian travel. I regretted the whole misplaced adventure.

Riding the spotless, punctual subway to my nightly "work" of pouring whisky and lighting cigarettes for drunken corporate types in gray suits, I used to look at the ads plastered above the passengers' heads. Even without reading Japanese, I could gather from the photos that they were advertising wedding parlors.

Everyone here seems to want to get married, I thought. Wouldn't there be someone wanting to marry *me*?

My desperation for the protection you used to provide—and which I had become addicted to—was reaching absurd heights. My one friend, an Iranian boy fleeing military service in his homeland, left to seek asylum in Canada. I was as lonely as one can be.

And then this tall, handsome, young Japanese man courting me, inviting me to share his tiny doll-house-like apartment, opening his home and heart to me. Kenji's English was almost nonexistent, but who cared? He took my coat to the dry cleaner, left the fridge stocked with frozen meals for me to have during his absence—took care of me. Exactly the medicine I so desperately craved. His family adopted me as if I were the lost orphan I already felt myself to be and soon thereafter became. I felt safe and protected among these strangers and, oddly, very much at home. We married in a Shinto temple. I opted for the most old-fashioned ceremony: the air perfumed with the scent of incense, lulled by the monotonous chant of the priests, with relatives from as far away as Aomori and Iwate prefectures attending, curious to see this rarity of a redheaded bride. One of the younger uncles even dared to kiss me on the cheek, showing off his worldliness and knowledge of foreign customs—not to mention guts—as astonished murmurs and embarrassed laughter spread around the room. No Japanese at that time would have kissed a woman outside the bedroom. I wore a golden *uchikake* (wedding kimono), lowered my head to take three teeny sips from the sake glass, listened to the marriage vows being read in a language that was meaningless chatter to me, took tiny steps proceeding to sign a long scroll with beautiful Chinese calligraphy exactly where I was told to, bowed when my groom silently indicated I should, sat back at my seat with a straight back, and kept my face as motionless as possible. I behaved impeccably, like a traditional Japanese bride, averting my eyes and smiling timidly. I had watched a video beforehand to know, literally, how to act.

An old school friend and two acquaintances I met at the karaoke club were my only invitees. I regaled in my anonymity, the "foreignness" being part of the charm. I was creating a new identity for myself, reinventing my history, erasing the pain of the past while shielding my offspring—one already swimming in my womb—from the dangers looming in their horizon. I had found the perfect camouflage to bring up my litter amid the former hunters. All of a sudden, even in my hopeless existence, a "future" tense seemed grammatically possible.

And I was liberated. In short—you weren't there!

Next came the trips to the obstetrician in Chiba, baby Mia, his late nights at the office spilling into after-work nightclubs.

New York was the next stop. Kenji, to my pleasant surprise, fitted in perfectly, making Manhattan his playground without missing a beat. Akasaka on the Hudson. Equally surprisingly, the one Hungarian word he picked up—*piszkos*, meaning "dirty" and relating to the laundry he sorted out together with you during your frequent and lengthy visits (yes, by then you had rejoined the picture)—sufficed for a perfect understanding and affectionate bond between you, even beyond the welcome and respect Japanese tradition required of him.

Was it love?

I was searching for an escape, and there was nothing more seductive than a faraway adventure, a place as remote as possible. There was so much to learn, to explore—tastes, textures, customs, literature, language. I was intoxicated. Our mutual exoticism saved us a lot of customary screening. We were both attracted to our ability to move from the conventional to a less restrictive reality, one that allowed more room for creative imagination. An overload of creative imagination, in fact. And that illusion worked. For a while. Until, eventually, familiarity gained ground and the bubble inevitably burst.

It turned into an ordinary marriage. Making a living. Family obligations, children, work, household chores pulling us apart. Paying rent, then paying a mortgage. He worked too hard. I was too lonely. He was too young. I was too tired. What else is new? A fight for power, a fight for freedom. A fight to survive. A constant pushing and pulling, unable to reach equilibrium. Marriage counseling. Good periods, good sex. Bad periods, no sex. Moving to the suburbs. Moving in the suburbs. A dog. Another baby. And on and on. Cut.

I made a little note to include here segments from my "divorce diary." That should be easy enough. Just type in the entries from those days when, after yoga classes, I proceeded in my beautiful 4x4 forest green Land Rover to the Red Lion Tavern, the only decent restaurant in our posh little town. I was not feeding my body. I hardly ate at the time. I nibbled on some nuts at the bar, my only nourishment for days, and downed one glass of red wine after the other. Later, half-drunk, I would scribble my thoughts in a little brown notebook. Though unaware of it at the time, I was preparing for the forthcoming separation.

I pick up the leather-bound pad, look at the yellowing pages, the irregular, familiar handwriting—but can't make myself read it, be reminded of it, to relive those days, even if only as a long-ago story. I gently place it back in the drawer to continue its silent hibernation. Over a decade later, it is still too painful to the touch. I will get to it in a while. Maybe.

Was it love?

Session 9
Night of All Souls
Tokyo, 1988

At three a.m. the phone rang. I was alone with three-week-old Mia. Our Tokyo apartment consisted of two rooms and a tiny entrance where our shoes were discarded and replaced with slippers before stepping in. A sixty-square-foot room functioned as the living and dining room. Sitting on soft cushions decorated with Mickey Mouse pictures, we ate our meals there, feet tucked under the low *kotatsu* table with the heater underneath warming them in the damp winters. The open "kitchen" consisted of a stove, a sink, a mini-refrigerator, and the obligatory rice cooker. The tiny bathroom had a small but very deep bath for which we had to warm the water manually by switching on a complicated electric system. Sliding doors led to the *tatami*-covered bedroom, also about sixty square feet, just enough for a futon to be pulled out from the closets and spread out for the night. Mia's miniature futon was next to ours. She was suffering from a congenital condition, her esophagus being too narrow and causing her to vomit her food, which meant that following hours of breastfeeding, my back aching and my arms numb, the still undigested milk would gush out in several intervals of warm jets, covering my shirt and hair and accumulating in a small puddle on the floor, while poor Mia's shrieks continued to pierce my already frazzled nerves.

Kenji was away in Osaka on business. I didn't even bother washing or attempting to clean myself from the layers of vomit. I was crying as desperately as my baby was. Exhausted, at the end of my wits, ready to do anything to stop the screaming, the incessant cycle of feeding and vomiting . . . then the sudden ring in the middle of that loneliest of nights.

My cousin's husband was on the very far end of the line, calling from Israel. He was clearly trying to save on the phone bill because he did not waste time on niceties, but rather chose a laconic: "Your father is dead."

Having performed his duty, he promptly hung up. I felt nothing, but continued crying and wishing for the baby to stop screaming, begging for sleep.

My father. That Hercules, the iron man of muscles, had started cracking some time before. By my last year of college, he was barely able to make his way—as usual, by bike—between his workshop and home. He kept going, fulfilling his obligation to pay my tuition fees through the end of my studies. Always a late riser, by then he would get in at noon and fumble around before heading home to the faithful bottle of vodka awaiting him at the foot of his favorite armchair.

What was he trying to escape? Was it the sight of his elder

brother being shot in front of his eyes, the body soundlessly dropping to quench the Danube's insatiable thirst for blood? The irrational, yet all the more powerful, guilt for having been helpless to save him? For having survived instead? Or was it the belated realization that he loved a wife who did not and could never love him, or anyone else for that matter? Was it disappointment over the meager rewards, if any, of father-hood? Or was it nothing but a simple genetic predisposition to alcoholism?

He became weaker and weaker, his legs starting to betray him. He was too weak to make it to my graduation ceremony from law school. And I was relieved. There was no way to hide my father's working-class background from my elite peers. On prior occasions, such as my piano recitals, he instinctively felt my discomfort—no words required—and declined to attend with one excuse or another. No further excuses were needed. He was shutting down.

There was a cost to trying to please the two women in his life. The exquisite food, the little gifts, the necklaces, bracelets, flowers, fur coat (for you), dresses (for me)—all that could not be accomplished on a metal worker's income unless he ignored the rules, took risks, was reckless to danger. The tax authorities never had any record of his existence. He was smarter than the system. Until the day the system caught up with him. No, he was never "discovered" by the regulators. The state never saw a cent of his money. But the lack of any of the social safety nets or medical insurance started to become a concern. An old wolf can no longer be a lone wolf. Aging required other tools, which my brave father never possessed. He sat on the terrace for long hours, his head held in his hands, his forehead wrinkled in thought. In a last effort, he managed to negotiate some social security payments in arrears and acquired minimal medical care, of which you would be the beneficiary for much longer than he was. And with that last breath, he let go, sold his work tools, gave up the lease on his shop, and parked the rusty bike for good.

Since I had always been his "little girl," we couldn't get to know each other the way two adults do, in a way that could have left behind lasting imprints. What do I know about the spoiled youth who was irresponsible enough to arrive late to the Seder night dinner? Apparently, the famous temper ran in the family, for, according to legend, my paternal grandfather welcomed his errant son by overturning the festive holiday table laden with all the dishes so meticulously prepared by the women of the house. Or about the young man, decked out in fashionable suits, who seduced one woman after another with his witty tongue? The pampered lover who spent his nights drinking and partying to be welcomed home to a hot bath drawn by his older, indulgent wife? The man who gave it all up, left with only a shirt on his back, and married you to forever try, but always fail, to melt your icy heart?

Whatever memories I have of him are tainted by your constant complaints, how you were the victim of his temper. I am sure it was true. I still remember his raging outbursts; Monika, you, and the six-year-old I was, escaping from our apartment through the balcony—we lived on the ground floor—moving about the neighborhood via back alleys, wondering whether or not it was safe to go back home. I used to feel like a hero, walking in first, knowing that he would never hurt me, his beloved. But as I grew, even I was no longer safe. My presence did not prevent him from—in a moment of temporary insanity—climbing up onto the railing of the terrace and threatening to jump. Was it cruel manipulation—as you scornfully observed—or were my desperate screams, coming from the darkest depths of anguish, the only means to pull him back to reality? First or secondhand impressions—madness layered by your own later lunacy.

He could never hide his disappointment in me for growing up. When it became impossible—despite the baby voice, giggles, silly jokes, and happy face. Impossible to hide that I was turning into a woman. Then I became "the whore." By that stage he was polishing off half a bottle of vodka a day, sipping from it throughout the evening, until eventually stumbling off to bed. I still pretended to be his little girl, tried to keep up the illusion for as long as I possibly could—hiding the bloody pads of my menstruations, still the best student in class, still his miracle child. But the mask had started cracking, bits and then larger pieces were crumbling down—the foundations were shaking—and I don't want to remember any more.

I did not see him for the last two years of his life. I don't know whether he missed me. Perhaps he was wrapped in a world far away from us, one to which the terminally ill withdraw. This last sentence is just a false justification in an attempt to clear my conscience for abandoning him. Not right away. For the first few years, I visited often enough. By then he could barely talk; his speech had become labored and almost incomprehensible. So he preferred to shut up. He was never one to make a fool of himself. I would push his wheelchair around the hospital grounds to catch some rays of sun. His arms, able to defeat young men in arm-wrestling contests even into his sixties, were by then shriveled to white bones covered with liver spots and marked by protruding blue veins, his nails too thick to cut. I shaved him with the old shavers, the type one needed to insert a razor into. I liked shaving him, stretching out the loose skin on his cheeks, caressing him with the blade, seeing the stubble give way to the smoothness below. When he could still talk, he said I was the best one at shaving him, better than the nurses. We continued our game of Daddy's little girl. My hand on his cheeks, it was our last act of love.

You later told me with extreme disgust how embarrassed you were to find out that, while he was in the hospital, half paralyzed and emaciated, skin and bones covered with bed-sores, with his one functioning hand my father had still managed to masturbate. I, on the contrary, find some conso-lation in the fact that even in that wretchedness he was able to squeeze one last drop of pleasure out of life. His spirit, the fighting essence in him, was not extinguished. That force that kept him running through the forests when hunted like a dog during the war, the willpower of the hedonist who enjoyed all vices—women, vodka, cigarettes, card games into the early hours of dawn—that force survived in him to the very end. I am grateful that he had that final pitiful crumb.

There were the goodbyes. Every time I left him in that hospital bed, one leg—the one that never stopped aching—slightly raised on a pillow, I would walk away backward, facing him until I reached the door. We would wave to each other, his skeletal hand moving slowly, until I could no longer see him as he disappeared behind the corner. Every single time, the same ritual. And every single time, I asked myself if I would see him again. So I concentrated all my energy on memorizing his face to imprint it into my cells, I concentrated all my love to pass it on to him with that gaze. Every single time, it was a mutual torture of love.

How do you know when is the last time? The last time you saw your hometown. The last time you made love to the man or woman you were in love with. The last time you said goodbye to a father who was fading away. When was it, finally, the last time I waved that long goodbye? I don't remember.

Because I left him.

You came to the airport to accompany me as I departed for New York, not knowing that it would be years before we were to see each other again. That by the time we did, I would be holding my own little girl in my arms.

I stayed in Queens for five months working, illegally, at a travel agency while taking a bar exam review course and dating seven different guys simultaneously. Permanently hungry, I was more interested in the menu than in any of my dinner companions. Unable to curb my—what would turn out to be a lifelong—addiction to adventure, I bought a ticket, packed my law books and two pairs of pants, made stopovers in Toronto and Vancouver, and landed in Tokyo on the 22nd of October. Almost a year to that date, the telephone rang at three a.m. local time to let me know that my father and I had indeed said our last goodbye.

That I had deserted him in his white hospital bed. That I had left him behind. That, true to my nature, I had pushed forward, headed for adventures wilder than the ones in his bedtime stories. That I was selfish. Yes, I'd admit to all that. I could not turn that hospital corner one more time. I could not watch his eyes, huge in that emaciated face, the desperation locked inside them, the bony arm waving as he disappeared behind the wall. So I escaped. I protected myself, and I would not apologize for it.

Where were you? Not only approving of my escape but actively encouraging it. Not only sending me, suitcase in hand, as far away as you possibly could, but as my father deteriorated and was facing imminent death, no one in the family—not Monika, my aunt, or my cousin—was allowed to inform me. No one was allowed to pick up the phone or write. And they all obeyed, fearing your wrath. You stood guard and protected me—as always—until the very last minute. Had you been able to spare me the information about his death, you certainly would have.

I did not go to the funeral. Mia was a newborn, still throwing up her food, and flights from Tokyo were a two-day ordeal; it was not practical. But that was not the only reason I stayed in our tiny apartment in Shibuya. It was, in part, the atheism I inherited from you. No afterlife, nothing left of the dead, so what is the point of going to see a body? It was the disregard I inherited from him as to what the rest of the world—family, friends, neighbors—would think. And it was too late. He was dead. The dead do not need visitors.

Session 10
Living with Shadows
New York, Early 1990s

The next stop on the escape route.

The twenty-sixth floor of a high-rise on the Upper East Side of Manhattan. I am sitting in the living room with the large windows overlooking the East River. We don't need any art to decorate the walls. The double north/east exposure provides a panoramic view of the magnificently blue waters sparkling like smooth glass on this sunny spring day. A few white sailing boats float gracefully down from Connecticut, an occasional cargo vessel, the turquoise bridge connecting Harlem to Queens on the other side. The traffic on the FDR below looks like a child's play set, with little toy cars moving to a soundless rhythm. This is an expensive view. All is tranquil and peaceful.

We left Tokyo less than two years ago, but we are already well acclimated to the American way of life. Mia is playing in her room. My husband is off in his midtown office. And I am sitting on the black leather sofa, in my preppy checkered skirt, the black stockings matching my sweater, my feet tucked into designer loafers. My classic yet somewhat artsy outfits draw admiring comments from the other "mothers who lunch" at the fashionable Park Avenue Methodist nursery school. I am sitting on the black leather sofa, hiding from the Nazis of fifty years ago.

I have built a life so entangled, so twisted and estranged from my past that one would, hopefully, be hard-pressed to follow the thread to its origins, to identify my daughter as concentration camp material. With her Japanese name and passport, born in Tokyo, her tall, handsome father with his Ermenegildo Zegna suit and elegant Asian features—his looks draw envious comments from fellow mothers—she should be far removed from danger as I know it. Because I will not allow another child of ours to fall into *their* hands. Not if I can help it—and I can, and I will. Instead, as I told my friend Ben— who flew over to attend my exotic wedding in Tokyo—pointing at my yet flat but soon to be inflated tummy, in a bitter paraphrase, "This is *my* solution to the Jewish problem."

I am joining the "bad guys," hiding in their midst. I am changing sides; I will not be the "good victim" anymore. I am protecting my kids—disguised in their tan Japanese complexions—the only way I know, from the dangers I already know. Alas, how would I detect the new, unfamiliar ones? Painstakingly, I acquire for them passport after passport— who knows which one may serve them best? I shuffle those passports at airports, searching for the right one for each particular journey, the Israeli usually hidden at the bottom of the pile. I am trapped in a nightmare that keeps reinventing itself, one danger dodged only to lead to another, even less predictable. I am finally entangled in a loop of fear that manifests itself in different forms and shapes, a web that keeps wrapping itself tighter around me; the harder I try to escape, the stronger its hold.

I protect my little girl but ultimately fail miserably to give her a sense of security. She, too, is contaminated. Ten years later, following the divorce from her father, twelve-year-old Mia and I tour the first house I would buy independently, the safe haven I end up securing for the three of us. By then Mia and I are protecting four-year-old Elise. The house would symbolize our recovery. We reach the basement level and the seller shows us a tiny crawl space made for the workmen's easy access in order to make repairs, the one we ultimately covered with a Jimmy Hendrix poster. Mia looks at me and smiles as if we are sharing a joke. When she speaks the words—"Perfect. We can hide here, in case . . ."—she echoes the very thought that runs through my mind.

In my desperation to provide her with security, all I have managed to do is pass on the disease. The joke is on me.

Why does an attractive redhead, who never knew a day of hunger in her life, look for the ghosts of Nazis on the faces of people she crosses on the streets of Tokyo and now New York? Why do her exotic, mostly Asian-looking daughters carry the virus?

"But you have not even been there," I was dismissed more than once by the non-Jewish men I attached myself to and to whom I tried, pathetically and obviously in vain, to convey the horror I draw in together with the air I inhale. I don't have an answer to that. Other than *blaming* you for the genetic transfer of the fear, the pain of what is by now an obsession. Yet, if I think about it, isn't obsession the only *normal* reaction? Could one have a four-year-old girl wearing a red coat and not fear? Could one have a four-year-old girl who is afraid of the dark, who is afraid of being forgotten in the supermarket, who is afraid of letting go of her mother's hand, and not remember all the little four-year-old girls with their hair neatly braided or curled, wearing their little red coats, holding their mothers' hands, obediently marching, like good little girls, to their deaths?

So, even though we live in New York, I religiously send my daughter to Japanese weekend school. I desperately want her to speak the language. She *must* be one of them—she must blend in. Even Kenji is puzzled, if pleased, by my enthusiasm. We attend all school performances, participate in the parent-teacher meetings, sing all the songs, bring rice balls to the picnics, watch the neat rows and rows of little ones, from the five-year-old kindergartners to the thirteen-year-olds standing in the courtyard on Sports Day, their innocent faces so trusting. I estimate in my head perhaps a thousand kids—multiply that number by how many courtyards of this size?—who were trusting in vain. And I cannot possibly contain the pain, the anger over the waste of so many unlived futures, unexpressed talents, lost hopes. The virtuosos who never learned how to play the violin, the writers who never learned how to read, the mathematicians who never learned how to count, the supreme court judges who never learned how to make a sentence, the doctors who never made their first checkup, the comedians who never told a joke, the athletes who never learned how to walk, the singers whose voices never matured beyond crying. And the gray German clerk who supervised the punctilious timetable of the trains taking them to a torturous death is spending quiet afternoons with his grandchildren and dog in a nondescript suburban house on the outskirts of Frankfurt, Munich, or Berlin, enjoying a respectable retirement, his only remarkable accomplishment in life reaching extraordinarily old age. The half-witted Polish train conductor who drove them to their destination is still drowning in his vomit every evening in the local bar. The young SS officer who barked them into the gas chambers is a loving father who, in turn, worries about his own children's below-average grades during parent-teacher conferences. That is what this world values and merits. And I am choking as I fight the tears, trying to hide them from my husband, standing next to me, who would be dreadfully embarrassed by his wife's inappropriate behavior in public, and from the other parents who would have no idea what had come over me, trying to save the mask of the woman I am supposed to be. I inevitably lose that battle.

And the pain I thought to have conquered, outwitted, is back with a vengeance. It rears its ugly head, unexpectedly, at all times. Twenty years later, in the French chapter of my life, during a typical winter vacation, we head off for a week at one of the fashionable resorts. I—miraculously on this earth as a result of the split-second decision when Dr. Mengele absentmindedly signaled you to the right, then miraculously having survived the contaminated needle administering a vaccine in communist Romania—am on a TGV loaded with the Parisian bourgeoisie heading to the slopes. I am seated on that train as if I, just like them, were destined to a quiet, calm life peppered with bucolic vacations. Any chameleon would be envious of my camouflage.

All the same, I get to enjoy the moments when the sun, the white mountain peaks, the blue skies, and the little chalets offering hot wine combine to produce something very close to perfect happiness. I am on the ski lift overlooking the white carpets of snow beneath. The ski instructor sitting next to me points to the silent, majestic beauty surrounding us, telling me this is the meeting point of the French and the Swiss borders, that we are now floating between the two countries. And I, in my warm ski gear, hat, sunglasses, and gloves, am seeing the desperation of those—at night on the snow and ice—carrying drugged babies on their backs. Hushing exhausted children. Hoping to reach the right side of the border, wishing for the snow to keep falling to cover their tracks from the hunters of human flesh. How many of them are buried right under these magnificent ski slopes? How many were caught and turned back? I chase those thoughts away, yet they persist. My ghosts claim their right to share life with me, *in* me. I drink hot wine at the next chalet. I drink hot chocolate at the resort. I make love to Jean-Marc. I dance at the club. I chase them away, but they hold tight, won't let me shake them off. And so we remain together, united in an eternal embrace.

I envy those who were born expecting that tomorrow is going to be another fine day, that the train always heads to the Alps and not to Auschwitz.

I live in parallel universes. Here and there. I walk the streets staring at the faces of passersby. I try to figure out a sign, a hint that would enable me to know whom I could trust, rely on in case I need to deposit my child for safekeeping. I search their faces for clues. The owner of the brasserie downstairs? The neighbor across the hallway? The pharmacist who smiled at me and seemed to have a kindly expression (or am I wrong)? Who would risk their own lives to save my daughter, and who would drag her by the arm straight to the nearest police station? There are both kinds walking every street— but how can one tell which is which? How can I tell which am I? And how can I tell which is my husband? There is no way to know, to *really* know. And how does one love? *Can* one love, with such doubt, imaginary or not, looming over our nuptial bed?

You transferred this heritage, together with all other nutrients, through the umbilical cord connecting us in your womb. I must have sensed an illusion of warmth in there; it may have even felt cozy, but it came at a price. Under the pretense of a normal pregnancy, a bloody transfusion was taking place, your DNA penetrating my brain and planting those memories in my every cell as if they were mine. I inhaled them as you exhaled next to me in the bed we shared throughout my childhood. You created me in your image to live your life even after you are gone.

Session 11

Pavements of Betrayal

Budapest, 2000

I land in Budapest and feel like a frog leaping back to its natural habitat, rejoicing to be splashing in its natal pond. As I hail a taxi and give directions to the driver in fluent Hungarian, he may notice a slight accent and a choice of some old-fashioned vocabulary rather than the modern slang, as if declaring, "My roots go deep." My father spent a big chunk of his youth in this city. At the time, the border between Hungary and Romania was quite porous, and one moved back and forth with ease. I was born into a more rigid era when not only East and West were clearly defined, but even within the Communist Empire, the divides were unyielding. Back in the 1970s, young men following global trends and sporting long hair were somewhat tolerated in Budapest, while such a *laissez-faire* attitude was unimaginable in Bucharest; the police would have given the offender a forced haircut (if lucky) or put him away for a few years in prison—a slightly more persuasive method of encouraging regular visits to the barber. The ten kilometers stretching between my birthplace that, postwar, became part of Romania and the Hungarian frontier represented the distance between alien universes. I never stepped on "officially" Hungarian soil until checking into the Hotel Gellért, famous for its thermal baths, and presenting an American passport.

Yet, my childhood was purely, if somewhat provincially, Hungarian. A relative's wife, who did not speak Hungarian, was referred to, behind her back, as "the Romanian." That "intermarriage" was a source of strain during the habitual Saturday night rummy-game soirees; for Anca's sake, the guests would brush up on the Romanian acquired during their school years—when it happened to be the official language in the region—but after a few laborious sentences they would fall, one by one, back into the homey, familiar mother tongue. Growing up, we spoke Hungarian at home long after immigrating to Israel, my brain switching gears to Hebrew as soon as I set foot outside the boundary of our apartment, diving instantly into the "modern" Israeli surroundings. It was a brave new world I was an integral part of, yet into which my parents did not stand a chance of entering. Hungarian was a language spoken by old relatives and family friends, a "sick" and "dying" language, ridiculed by the arrogant Israelis. I was the butt of jokes when my friends accidentally overheard me speak it with my parents. It was the language of the pale and weak, the crippled and maimed, the scorched leftover of European Jewry, weaklings collapsing onto Israeli shores. So when I arrive in Budapest thirty years later, I am amazed to hear cool blonde girls in skinny jeans cheerfully chatting away in the language of the dead.

Budapest fits like a glove. The food offered in the street stalls and restaurants emits the same odors that used to greet me as I stepped into your kitchen after a long day at school. The casual conversations and expressions are identical to those that accompanied the endless shuffling of Rummikub tiles in our old living room, serving as lullaby to my childish ears. I just want to sink into the comfortable, soft blanket of familiarity and breathe a sigh of relief.

In Budapest, I suddenly see you in a new light. In Israel, you are still an "immigrant," out of place. For all practical purposes, you are deaf, mute, and illiterate; since the time I entered second grade and learned how to read, you and my father have been asking me to translate documents for you. In Budapest, you are comfortable. You don't draw a second glance. I am not embarrassed by you; having an old, bitchy Hungarian mother is the norm. I take you to the theatre and don't have to whisper an abbreviated version of what is happening onstage in your ear. At a restaurant, you can read the menu and order on your own, without my having to be the middleman between you and the waiter. The Hungarian Gypsy musicians, expecting a generous tip, know precisely what song they should play to your liking. You ask the hotel clerk for the keys and find your way to our room. You, my mother, for the first time in my life, *fit in*. I feel like an ugly duckling who has discovered she is not a duckling at all; she is the daughter of a regal Hungarian swan, white crown of feathers and all.

But just as I want to relax into that *gemütlich* homeyness

I feel like someone returning to her childhood apartment to find that strangers have claimed it as their own and are using her most private belongings, that the comfortable, safe familiarity is an illusion. Budapest is anything but home; it is the heart of danger! We, actually, are on a pilgrimage to the family cemetery.

Crossing the bridge over the beautiful blue Danube, I stop to stare at the tiny waves dancing on its surface. My uncle's remains lie still, resting in the soiled waters. My father and you agreed on one thing only—you made a pact to protect me. So my father, faithful to your sacred accord, never mentioned that night. His one reference to the war was about the time he tried to steal across the border to the relative safety of Romania. Exhausted, having walked all night under cover of darkness, he discovered at the first light of dawn that he had been going in circles and ended up at his starting point; he was still on Hungarian reclaimed land. Forty years later, the whole episode, as he relayed it, sounded rather comical.

My father's cousin, Gyuri, used a similarly lighthearted tone when telling me about a luckier escape. Like most young Jewish men, they were both ordered by the Hungarian Arrow Cross fascists (*Nyilaskeresztes Párt*) to join the infamous "labor service" brigades. Hardly any of the recruits survived the forced exertion in mines and quarries, the marches into mine fields—used as an efficient way to clear them before the advancing German troops—the horrid conditions and torture. Gathered on the platform, waiting for the train that would transport them to their pitiful destiny, my father, nonchalantly smoking a cigarette, strolled to the other end of the tracks and hopped onto a train heading in the opposite direction. Gyuri's voice was still filled with awe at such brazenness:

"Can you believe it? He had guts! Walking casually, a hand in his pocket, as if promenading on the central Vaci Street! Poof, he was gone."

I couldn't forget that lesson. It had already been imprinted in my genetic code:

"Be ready. Alert. Watch for every opportunity . . . In order to survive, one has to be on the move."

In December 1944, weeks before the "liberation," the hunt for Jews only intensified. Ilonka, lover and later gratitude bride, hid my father in her basement. With him were his brother, Sandor, and several of their cousins—including the sixteen-year-old Bondi. Ilonka's brother, a member of the Hungarian Arrow Cross militia, informed the authorities. Their hiding place uncovered, the doomed men were tortured all night, disfigured beyond recognition, and by early dawn, their hands tied together behind their backs, were marched in pairs to the banks of the Danube to be executed. Lili, Sandor's fiancée, getting the news of her beloved's final hour, died of grief a few months later. My father, the "black sheep" of the family, survived. Under cover of darkness, slowly untying the rope binding his wrists, he freed his arms. Watching the first row of men, including his brother, being shot, he realized he had nothing to lose. At his turn to stand in line in front of the rifles pointed at them, he sprinted ahead. The bullets whistling past his ear, he tumbled, fell to the ground, and lost consciousness. The hunters, believing him dead, resumed the killing. By the time my father came through, with only his hearing impaired, and made his way back to Ilonka's relieved embrace, the remainder of the group was lying at the bottom of the famous river.

How many degrees of exponentiation, X squared (no, not enough), X cubed, X raised to the nth power, did it require for one young man, in his prime, to be lucky enough to make it out—scarred, but alive? What chance did the studious, intellectual Sandor have? Young Bondi, in the spring of his youth?

We are at home and strangers. Had events taken a couple of different steps, had the Allies won the war a few months earlier, I would have proudly considered myself "European." We would have spent our weekends and summer vacations on my great-grandparents' estate leading a leisurely existence. You could have helped me with my homework instead of blanking out in front of pages filled with strange letters written from right to left. You could have clearly explained to your doctor what was ailing you instead of trying to converse with him in sign language. I would have been proud of my beautiful mother rather than embarrassed by an inadequate outsider. (How much injustice have I caused you with that childish embarrassment? How could I make it up to you—knowing that, given the benefit of a second chance, I would have behaved just as badly?)

Enraged, I try to hate the taxi driver, I try to hate the vendor at the ticket office. I try *so* hard to hold on to that hate—but I can't. On the contrary. I am seduced by the smiley faces, by the familiar expressions of endearment all around me, the cashier at the store calling me *szivem*, "my heart," when she hands over my new purchase. I melt to the core.

Seder night. We celebrate our escape from the past, the suffocating memories, the "tradition," by choosing the opposite of a Jewish festivity. At a restaurant on the outskirts of the city, we are feasting on pork chops and listening to a Gypsy band playing your favorite songs. The kitsch oozes from the walls, but that is perfectly fine. You are in a good mood, singing along with the screeching violin as it plays the old tunes your admirers serenaded you with, the ones you taught me as we strolled home together, hand in hand, from my piano lessons. The sugary words are still timely in the realm of the crisp Budapest air: *A zongorámon ott áll még a képed, ez az egy maradt meg, semmi más . . . milyen furcsa is a sors: mikor ezt adtad nekem, még nagyon boldog voltál énvelem.* (Your photograph still rests on my piano. It's the one remainder, nothing else . . . how strange is fate: when you gave it to me, we were still so very happy.)

Surrounded by heavy wooden tables overlaid with hand-embroidered tablecloths, painted ceramic plates hanging on the walls, and clouds of paprika-infused fumes filling the air, you travel down memory lane, back to the days you were the "village beauty." Your once-black curls have turned into a silvery crown, some wrinkles are penciled in to mark your forehead, but you are nonetheless beautiful—your cheeks smooth and luminous and your eyes brilliant black diamonds filled with tears of joy.

I have never seen you as happy. Just the two of us, breaking all the rules. Buying endless treats at the Easter fair—childhood favorites you have not tasted in over fifty years. You are chatting with every stranger as if to make up for all the mute years lost in the wastelands of Hebrew. If people are supposed to be less energetic with age, you never heard of that rule. You are more alive than ever, exhausting me with your vigor, ready to go on and on day and night.

But I can sense your apprehension. We are at once at home and on enemy territory. A home that has brutally rejected us—yet one we, betrayed children, still long for; aching to be cuddled in its embrace; to let go of the memories, of the "duty" to remember, the obligation to those who never made it out. We just want to forget, to turn time back. In vain.

We frolic about and play, blindfolding ourselves to the past. Only years later do I hear the story—and by then it is not told by you.

Session 12

Divorce

Westchester, New York, Late 2001

It was the lowest point in my life. I would have been willing to sign anything just to be out of that courtroom. A broken woman, barely able to recite my name at the request of the court stenographer, feeling like a caged animal in that mediator's office, mocked and humiliated. Utterly defeated.

You understood. You went through a divorce—which was far less acceptable at the time—from your uncle/husband. When things turned ugly, as they always do, you didn't have a therapist by your side to consult with or to prescribe you antidepressants. In lonely despair, you opted for the do-it-yourself solution; you climbed to the attic, a bottle of pills already emptied into your stomach. Had the maid missed your wavering silhouette, this story would never have been written.

As soon as the man stepped out, there was a lacuna for you to fill. Worried as you were prior to my divorce, trying to dissuade me from going ahead, fearing for me, as always "protecting" me—the moment the matter became a *fait accompli*, you turned into my loudest and steadiest cheerleader. With your nuclear-power-plant force of determination behind me, I soon not only emerged from the ruins but dared to aim for an even better life than before: a bigger house in a better neighborhood, a more luxurious car, designer clothes, lavish vacations. You unearthed in me a force that must have been there all along, except that I was not aware of its magnitude; courage you never possessed but, reluctantly, identified in your younger daughter. A force you initially tried to suppress in me:

"You are far too boisterous."

"You are *so* argumentative. It's unbecoming a young lady!"

"Why don't you adopt more feminine manners?"

Those rebukes had been trickled into my ears since I was keeping you company on the kitchen floor, playing doctor (not nurse) with my dolls.

But now the gloves were off. You encouraged me to unleash that verve with a vengeance and conquer the world. What you could never do in your own life—be an active player rather than a passive object to be played with—you now delegated to me. In me you had finally recognized the tool to execute a revenge on a universe that had thus far ill-treated you. And you wouldn't let them do the same to me.

It wasn't easy. When I came home exhausted from long hours of conference calls, meetings, negotiations, office politics, was worn out by Mia's teenager crises, too tired even to enjoy Elise's broad smiles and fat, sticky hugs—you were on the other end of the telephone line, pouring courage into my ears. Your criticism filed away, you were full of praise, backing me all the way. Once again, I was your *gyongy viragom* and *csilag fenyem*—my almost forgotten terms of endearment. And an infusion of love was transmitted through the copper undersea wires, providing me with essential nutrients.

For a while, we were a team. A team determined to steer this fragile boat and the children on board to a safe harbor. We were partners. When I felt blinded by fatigue and unable to think, you were the captain and I the crew, executing your advice. But most of the time, we were just together, hand in hand, navigating our family of four—two women, one close to middle age, one actually old, and two little girls—in rough seas. You and I were divided by an ocean, yet we rowed in tandem and were as close as can be. And there was no power that could have stood in our way.

Session 13
Solitude

Your presence is a permanent companion, and I conduct a nonstop dialogue with you in my head. As if the loneliness that you complain about in each and every one of our telephone conversations has entrapped me as well. I need your echo to resonate within the walls of my skull.

How do you spend those unending hours with no one to talk to, imprisoned within the confines of your apartment? Even with your cleaning mania, how long can you keep yourself busy before all the sinks are glittering white and carpets scrubbed of any hint of dust? Watching television must have its limits too . . . my twice-a-day telephone calls surely do not suffice.

You are resourceful. Designing and sewing your clothes, you stitch them all by hand, half seated in your throne of a bed. The neat stitches so sweetly praised by your own mother— one of the few memories you still retain of her after your violent, forced separation—turned out to be a lifelong occupation. One precise little stitch follows the other, progressing patiently; you haven't the faintest idea that such skills could have earned you a fortune had you employed them at Dior, for example. It helps you kill time.

For most of my childhood, you were a "stay-at-home mom." That was the norm in our social milieu. The house chores—shopping for food, cooking, washing dishes, laundry, ironing, changing the bedding, wiping the dust, washing the floors (daily), and on and on—kept you busy from dawn to late evening. You woke me up, helped me dress, carried my school bag as you accompanied me to school, waited for me with a warm meal at lunchtime, sat by my side while I did my homework, your hands never resting, always knitting or mending. You had hardly time for a friend's visit or a chat. Or for being a grandma to Monika's children. You were still a young woman at heart. Only years later did I understand that our frequent shopping trips to the Bambino shoe store on Bialik street in Ramat Gan, which created a lifelong "shoe habit" in me, had less to do with my growing feet and more with the silver-haired, handsome store owner.

Following my father's death, passionate flirtations during dance parties in various Golden Age Clubs provided welcome distraction and fertile landscape for intrigues. But all that is in the past. Your social contacts have diminished to the occasional girlfriend, the one you happen not to be on bad terms with at the moment. Old suitors no longer call. Monika won't even pick up the phone—it's her turn to revenge whatever grudges she holds. How do you protect yourself from losing your mind?

* *

Many years ago, an associate at the time with a mega-large, prestigious law firm, I was about thirty-four or five. No kid by any standard. I was asked to fly over on one of those frighteningly tiny planes to Portland, Maine, to perform due diligence on one of the ski companies operating in the area. I was shut for three days in a room filled with corporate binders, looking into minutes from board meetings, analyzing debt structures. I was pretty much lost. There was no way to really read, let alone comprehend, all that documentation. During the day, I did my best to decipher the hundreds of binders piled up in the windowless room, taking notes no one would ever look at, and missing my daughter. At night, I wandered alone in the streets of Portland, dining solo in restaurants, ordering lobster (what else?) while trying to stay within the reasonable limits of the expense account. Even later at night, I would still be wandering the streets of Portland, looking for a friendly bar. A woman alone, too strange a sight for the local bums to harass.

And even later, alone in my hotel room—a group of rowdy college kids or a rock band on a bad night would not have left the room in the state the maid found it the next morning. The little sample alcohol bottles from the minibar were strewn all over the place, snack wrappers littering every corner, the bed all messed up following vigorous masturbation to the tune of one of the porn channels. It was a night of angst, of destructive oblivion.

That anxiety did not subside over the years. Other

business trips followed suit. I had to pay cash in one of the London hotels to compensate for and hide the fact that in my drunken state I had vomited on the rug in the room, ruining it. Oftentimes, when both my daughters are away on school trips or sleeping over at a friend's house, my evenings are filled with chaotic little vices: overdrinking, overeating, over-something, waiting to collapse semiconscious in bed by two or three or four o'clock in the morning, too numb to feel anything.

The next mornings are usually calm. The nightly demons have been chased away by the light. The ghosts are back in the shadows. Other than the occasional nausea or headache, I can hardly remember the events of the previous evening. I promise myself never to repeat such toxic behavior. And, for a couple of months, I don't.

I feel abandoned. You passed down to me your deep-rooted fears and kept the only key to unlock the cabinet that held the antidote to their effect; you possess the elusive magic words to dispel them. You made me as dependent on you for survival as if our veins were inosculated.

But now you are mute. That conspiracy of silence that you and my father so carefully guarded has turned into a jail, its walls impossible to penetrate or break down. Neither of us is able to open up those vaults of memory and air the pain. And without you by my side, I have to face all those memories, which are not my own—black-and-white pictures of horror— alone. You are experiencing the same on your end, but I can't pick up the phone to call. That lifelong taboo is stronger than us. Unable to comfort each other, we are locked in our respective bedrooms. Loneliness turns into anxiety, panic, madness.

I blind myself with alcohol, I look for oblivion in chaos, I exhaust myself to win a moment of forgetfulness. Love affairs, relationships, marriages are Band-Aids. They partially cover the wound. Solitude is not as evident within their walls; they provide a temporary sense of belonging. Preparing for your departure, you are desperately looking to entrust me in the hands of another man. Meanwhile, I continue limping on. My days are a balancing act—making sure there are enough distractions and hedonistic pursuits on one end of the seesaw to prevent me from sliding into the abyss on the other.

Session 14

Back Alleys Leading to Main Street

Corsica, Summer 2003

First it was a casual one—well okay, two—night stand, a quickie to chase away the ennui. We were both experts in the game of seduction. He saw an "American" and was intrigued. Picked an alley in an old village in Corsica to "accidentally" bump into me and asked if I'd like my picture taken. The oldest trick in the book. I could see sophistication was not part of the program. Of course, I wanted my picture taken. I followed with a compliment about his fluent English, which he readily accepted without suspecting the slightly phony nuance. I was rather bored by the tired, old banter but, out of obligation to my nature, was unable to refuse a turn in the game. I slept with him just to add another checkmark on the list of conquests or whatever it was. So did he. Two disillusioned, blasé, overly used and scratched middle-aged adults.

Those cynics, of course, make the best romantics, the banal raw material for fate to toy with. After a couple of mildly satisfying sexual encounters and a few tongue-in-cheek pleasantries, we were supposed to part at Orly airport, shelving this short episode and each other's names with the many other anonymous additions to the catalogue of affairs.

However, as I was walking to the Avis car rental desk, I stopped and followed his silhouette still visible through the glass wall. As he hailed a taxi without so much as looking back, a bittersweet melancholy—together with a certain knowledge that one day we would be together again, which I, of course, immediately dismissed—was, hesitantly but most definitely, lingering in my mouth. A week later we went on a date and made love for the first time. The previous times were mere fucks. As I softly kissed his forehead when we lay holding each other, I could feel the surprise flowing like an electric shock through his body, as if the barrenness of his skin had forgotten the possibility of rain. And I caressed him, rediscovering tenderness buried so deep inside me that by then it felt almost foreign.

His email three days later took me by surprise. I sat at my desk, back in my New York office, staring at the screen and rereading the laconic message several times. I then responded with a much longer email and spell-checked my reply. An exchange ensued, in which we each tried to outwit, impress, and discover the other. I think we, both addicts of the written word, actually fell in love with our own mastery of the medium and ability to perform rather brilliantly, the other just providing a ready audience or perhaps a mere mirror to our respective vanities.

But *der mentsh trakht un Got lakht* (man plans and God laughs), as they say in Yiddish. Not that he would have had the faintest idea what Yiddish was at the time—I was probably the first Jewess he had ever dated. We had fallen victim to our own trap. Our tricks worked better than we, their creators, intended them to. Within less than a month we were in love, at least in theory. And soon thereafter, the actual sex we had during our sporadic transatlantic visits with one another was already spiced and well primed by erotic emails flying back and forth. Steamy fantasies written in the height of sexual longing experienced by a ripe forty-something-year-old woman, sent to a man of a certain age, clearly flattered by his ability to still generate such passion.

But there must have been more. Some secret ingredient that made the longing so desperate, a mysterious language that only the body can decipher. Therefore, after three years of increasingly imaginative erotic correspondence, speckled with a somewhat milder version of actual activity from time to time, the moment came to put all that theory into a laboratory and experiment with real life. I quit my job. Packed my house. Boarded the plane for a one-way flight to Paris.

You were with us on that fateful vacation in Corsica. You saw him fleetingly at the communal restaurant of the resort passing by, carrying his lunch or dinner—and were not impressed. It would take years—it would take the relationship turning into a formal "marriage"—for you to give it your blessing.

You were with us at the wedding. With your last strands

of strength, you managed the flight, danced the floor away, and played the role of the "mother of the bride" to perfection. You were in your element—the Queen Mother. Mia took advantage of the festive occasion and, in the most touching of gestures, went on stage and played a brilliant czardas which, she announced, was, "dedicated to my grandmother."

For that one day, the magic returned. You were my admirable, beautiful, and loving mommy again—giving away your little princess like in the fairy tales of my childhood. As if you believed in them. As if you didn't know better . . . as if you didn't foresee the outcome. You could have given Meryl Streep acting lessons.

Life continued, but the show could not. You felt your powers waning and started losing confidence in your ability to protect me for much longer. For lack of alternatives, you forced yourself to put your trust in the illusion, looked to this husband to serve as a replacement. It was still a flimsy prospect, but you wouldn't have been able to shut your eyes without it, so you convinced yourself that he was my knight in shining armor. You handed me over—desperately trying to tell him in Hungarian, accompanied by gestures, "Please take good care of her."

Hoping that this random choice, this accidental sexual encounter that turned into love that turned into marriage would survive and, against all odds, prove to be the right one to replace you as my guardian angel. Even if you have to let go of life, you can't possibly let go of that hope.

Session 15
Duel

I am still lying on him, my soft, warm blanket of flesh wrapping his body. My torso is longer than his. We breathe evenly in perfect synchronization. His hand in my hair, messing it up. He delicately taps on my shoulder, signaling me to release him from this enveloping prison of my body that is closing on his gaunt, slight, and bony frame under me. He ages well, still a potent lover. He has never been manly in the stocky way of firm muscles and wide shoulders. He was always fragile and slightly built, delicate against my resilience. Nevertheless, there is strength and stubbornness in that weakness. His roots are firmly planted in this ground and flow down to his offspring in a decisive stroke. Just as my indestructible façade hides the vulnerability of one who would never belong—past, present, future.

So our paths cross in a moment of tenderness after lovemaking. Most times our distance is on the surface, in our face and undeniable. And yet, there are those very rare but nonetheless miraculous moments when we touch. It is more than most are blessed with. Even two dimensions are better than none.

Here we are then, two—no, not broken but seriously damaged—used goods that we are. Our rough edges are polished by wear and tear. He is graying; I am heavier around the tummy. We share an illusion of closeness, a fleeting moment with a lingering taste of sweetness in my veins. He approaches our lovemaking with hesitation, as if an indulgence one should not abuse. It does not take long for the intimacy to become too much for him to bear, too intimidating. And he is back at his computer, covering—in his dry, technical way—the momentary emotional nakedness with a thin cloth called "rationality." As if reading academic articles provides him safe grounds to step on, relieves him of the insecurity and embarrassment of revealing his loneliness and neediness to another person.

I stare at the fly trapped in the chandelier. Now aware of and embarrassed by the twenty pounds of overweight I am wrapped in, I quickly dress. Yet the waves of pure corporal satisfaction make me yield easily to the sofa that is ready to support my body, arms and legs stretched sideways, floating. Unlike him, I am at peace with my earthly pleasures. Free of Catholic guilt, I bask in sensual delight, letting my body dictate and needing no pretense of "intellectual" disguise to cover my nude desires. While he is searching for and believes in a "truth"—I know there is none. There is no kindness, no logic, no order, no God. There is nothing for me to look for beyond an ultimate death and plain void. In the interim, who could blame us for seeking oblivion in what is possible?

Love as the perfect means of distraction. An illusion of pleasure, sometimes forced, but almost never failing. Yes, I use our bodies; I am mechanical and pragmatic about it. He sometimes intuitively senses my motives and resents being employed in my deceit. He usually ends up cooperating, though—I have become quite skilled in the art of seduction. But I deceive only myself.

I start knowing him. It's only a start. He needs to be tenderly coerced, cajoled to love. We study each other's bodies, minds, and preferences to utilize them for our needs. We call it love. And maybe it is.

He is older. Resigned to accept some of my willful ways in an effort to secure some peace and stability in the coming years. Those are foreign words to me. Why did he take such a gamble, place the security of his most vulnerable years in the hands of a nomad? In the hands of a woman who has no country, no God? It's a strange bet. Was he, the equilibrated man, the rational scientist, being a bit self-destructive? Or did he sense that only one as needy as I am will forever be bound to him by the cord of that want? He knew that—for lack of any other faith—I would be faithful to *us*. That he can provide me with the solid ground to step on, an escape from the abyss. And that I would be grateful for land after a very lonely journey on rough seas. That I would need his eyes to be my lighthouse. In exchange, I would offer him my strength. I would be his rock to lean on. My soft flesh would warm him on dark, wintery nights. It was a fair enough trade. So he took a leap of semi-calculated risk.

We eye each other with suspicion; we circle around each other like two boxers measuring up each other's strength, keeping vigil, trying to predict our opponent's next move, looking for a vulnerable opening, waiting for the right moment to strike. We respect each other. There is a balance—not exactly of fear but of awareness of the other, alertness to the other, continuous consideration of the other. Consideration in both senses of the word.

It makes for a tiring marriage, but we both need that challenge—he needs it for the blessed distance it provides, and I for the blessed distraction. So we allow ourselves only a few unguarded minutes to rest our arms, under the disguise of sex, to take a deep breath and then dive back into our little domestic battlefield filled with sarcasm and witticism. And I look at his face, the face of a complete stranger. And I am beautiful in the mirror of his eyes, changing hats, outfits, costumes, disguises for an audience of one.

Our story is being written as we go along.

Session 16
Loss of Innocence

Sex is almost taboo between mothers and daughters. Other than the "obligatory" explanation somewhere around puberty about the flowers and the bees, it is left to an occasional courageous biology teacher to broach the subject or delegated to a group of embarrassed peers to exchange rumors and half-truths. Once a young woman takes a few steps toward having her own experiences, it hardly comes up in conversation with her mother. Certainly not in the direction of mother-to-daughter professions. And never in the form of an aging mother confessing sexual desire.

As always, you made your own rules.

You were quite prudish. At least that was the image you conveyed at the time I was young and you were still with my father. I found your complaints about him imposing himself on you— far too often, according to you—embarrassing and breaching a boundary that I would much rather you had kept. According to you, he was behaving like an animal, as obsessed and excessive about the sexual act as you were repulsed and disgusted by it. You only fulfilled your domestic "obligation" to appease him and, quite often, as the only means to soothe his explosive temper. You sneaked into his bed—you didn't share one—when you were in need of his goodwill for an occasional larger-than-usual purchase, a new washing machine or sofa. But, as a rule, you were frigid in the old-fashioned way that was considered appropriate for a "respectable woman" of your milieu. Sex was a duty, a favor or a reward a wife offered her husband. A "dirty" activity. There were exceptions; you mentioned confessions made by a couple of close friends, who shyly admitted to actually enjoying the act of lovemaking. Your reaction to their wanton ways shifted—depending on your mood—between disbelief, curious envy, mild amusement, and disdain.

You didn't try to pass that attitude on to me. On the contrary. In me, you encouraged a total sexual liberty, almost promiscuity, as if you were trying to make up, through your daughter, for your own inhibitions and inability to enjoy erotic love. You were a trusted coconspirator whenever we had to lie to my father about my whereabouts—inventing sleepovers at girlfriends' far beyond the age it would have made sense. And when, in the spirit of total openness between us, I called you following my first full intercourse—"Mom, it happened!"—you were as nonchalant as if I'd reported having gone to the movies.

"Oh, well. Has it, indeed? What time are you coming home?"

You told me you were glad that I didn't turn out to be as "cold" as you were.

"Luckily, It must've been your father you took after," you concluded—still with a slight air of self-virtuous superiority.

It was only after his death, following your stay with us in New York, that you started opening up to pleasure. Not yet with a real-life flesh-and-blood man. It was my first husband's idea that we buy you a manual massage device. We were walking up Third Avenue, and on the left side of the street, right opposite Bloomingdale's, was a store that specialized in such equipment. Massagers were popular in Japan, and he thought using one could relieve the chronic back pain that was debilitating you for days at a time. Only a couple of years later, when I got a phone call from you telling me the machine had broken down, insisting I send you a replacement *as soon as possible*, did I realize by the urgency in your voice that you must have discovered its off-label uses.

It would be another five years, when you met a man of Iraqi origins with whom you could exchange but a few broken sentences—he spoke not a word of Hungarian and your Hebrew still left room for improvement—before you whispered to me, "I *finally* know what it means to be physically attracted to a man! When he touches me, I shiver . . ."

The affair did not last long. Not with your temper tantrums and suspicions that it was your "palace" of an apartment he was after rather than you. Perhaps you were right. Whatever his motives, you kicked him out within a couple months of living together, and that was the end of your first and last attempt at carnal passion.

I am fairly certain those later years revealed but the tip

of what could have been the opposite of an iceberg, a volcano that must have been wasting away in the depths of your body, under all the layers of "propriety" drilled into women of your generation. And when you finally found the courage to let go of that false morality—well, it was late. Too late.

I cry for you, my sensual and warm mother. I cry for your innocent desire being suffocated before it had a chance to bud, sacrificed in beds of men who brutally crushed it to reach their own selfish gratification. Who, hardened by their own tragedies, were blind to your virginal purity and treated it with coarse hands and rough souls. No wonder your petals closed shut. That after those frightening, lonely nights, bruised and aching, squashed under the weight of your tormentor—who happened to be your uncle as well as your much older first husband—no man was allowed to get near your delicate core. No man could ever again penetrate through the thick walls of bitterness and resentment you built for protection. The only physical tenderness you allowed yourself was with me.

A wasted life.

Session 17

Touch

Until not so long ago, I used to take baths with Elise. Scrubbing her thick black hair and then rinsing it, making sure all remains of shampoo had been washed off. Those were our most intimate moments—the sacred ritual of cleansing, sharing our femininity, mine fully ripe soon on the edge of decline, hers barely budding. She was still young enough to be naked in front of her mom without embarrassment, no pubic hair in sight, her breasts as yet nonexistent. Still young enough not to feel awkward sharing the tub with Mommy, lying back, her head resting on my thighs as I gently passed my fingers over her peach-perfect skin, taking care not to let any of the soapy bubbles hurt her eyes. She was still young enough to look at me seriously and say, "Mom, you are the most beautiful woman in the world"—and mean it.

That same fleeting closeness which I used to share, a bit longer ago, with Mia—which I wish I could lock in a bottle to open and relive when I am older, say, your age—I feel it flickering away. I am holding onto the tail end of moments that are already lost in time. I am missing what I still had just a few baths ago. When my skin is wrinkled, my stomach a soft ball of fat, my pubic hair thinning, my legs a landscape of thick distorted veins. When touching me will be something my daughters dread rather than crave. I will then need the memory of their warmth to soothe my pain.

I used to have that physical intimacy with you. We so naturally took a bath together at the end of the day. I combed your hair—long, some strands of gray already parting the jet-black mane—and had my head in your lap as you washed my sunny-red curls. Our conversations were effortlessly floating like the tiny movements of the soapy, balmy water we were immersed in. I was, perhaps, eight or nine years old.

"Why do you have hair between your legs, Mommy? Can I see?"

"Stop," you replied in a bit of discomfort. "I am just like you."

I looked down. I was all smooth and my skin the same color as everywhere else on my body.

"No, it's not like mine. Your *pina*"—the word we used for your genitals whereas mine were *nuna*, in childish Hungarian—"is hairy and red. I want to see."

"It's the same. There's nothing to see."

"I want to see!"

You resigned and spread your legs for a quick second to immediately close them shut. Your voice turned firm.

"Now you saw and leave me alone."

My curiosity not quite satisfied, I knew further insistence

would lead nowhere. Soon distracted by some soapy bubbles you blew by making a circle between your thumb and your index finger, we slowly moved on to other topics.

The last few years, I hardly touch you. Even on our rare meetings. On my most recent visit, you asked me not to kiss you, as if the cancer were contagious. I readily obeyed. Occasionally, you would pass a tentative finger along my arm, caressing it back and forth. No more. As if old age were a disease that the young should stay away from. You never had an aging parent to relate to, an example to follow. You never saw your own mother old, then dying of natural causes; no one was there to show you the way. Unlike death, aging existed only in the abstract. You are on *terra incognita*, making up your own rules. And they are strict to the touch.

What if I had insisted? What if I had just wrapped my arms around you and given you a real kiss, not a peck on your hair, but a kiss right in the center of your shiny, smooth cheek? The way I used to when I was little. But I never do. You asked me to offer you perfumes as presents, suspecting you may be carrying that distinct scent old people wear as a second layer of skin. In fact, you never did. Still, I refrain from kissing you. I let the distance be. And I think of the love, almost passion, exhibited by my daughters toward me. And I remember how passionately I loved you when I was their age. How eager I was to learn the old Hungarian love songs you taught me on the way home from my piano lessons, to hear your stories about princesses wearing light blue crinoline dresses and tiaras heading to their first ball, how I believed in your powers and wisdom—and I wonder how all of that faded into the faint hug that I nowadays give you from time to time. How did we get from there to here? I know it is as inevitable as the passage of time. That someday my little Elise will most likely find me an old burden, wonder why on earth one would want to continue living in such a state (the gross soft ball of fat called a stomach, the distorted veins, the large brown liver spots on my face and hands). She may not quite feel disgust but something not completely removed from it either.

And I already feel the pain and regret.

December 15

*T*he narrow window of tenderness has shut before it even had a chance to properly open. Your voice on the phone is again shrill and demanding. I had to promise to take you to the hospital for a checkup as soon as I arrived. In your frustration and self-delusion, you blamed me for not getting there soon enough. You told me that I wished you dead to shorten my own difficulties caring for you—the accusation had some truth in it and hurt exactly where you aimed the arrow. You blamed me for having wished you dead for the inheritance, which was not true but hurt nonetheless. Your voice was weak, yet you managed to insult and accuse and cause havoc in my heart even while imprisoned in your bed. I wavered between endless pity and pure hate.

I have not departed yet, and you are already questioning whether I would wake up early enough to bring you your coffee to bed at exactly seven o'clock in the morning. Would I wash the glasses well enough or leave them as dirty as you suspect me capable of? You insist that when I go out, I must be back as soon as possible.

I try to negotiate along the undersea optic fiber, but I feel my feeble arguments falling on deaf ears. You tell me in an agitated voice that all you require is peace and quiet, and I am upsetting you already.

"Don't even come if you intend to be so impatient," you bark—as if I had a choice—and promptly hang up.

I know the rules of the game but still fall into the trap each and every time with my eyes and heart wide open. I suspect you may even manipulate the severity of your condition. You usually seem to "revive" as soon as I land at your doorstep. I, who last night could not stop the tears flowing at the thought of losing you, am now wishing for your speedy death. Hell, I even start contemplating how to speed it up—perhaps by putting pills in your drink—and scare myself at the mere thought of it. I start having stress symptoms. I go to bed exhausted to wake up an hour later, unable to shut my eyes again. Around four-thirty a.m. I manage to doze off, only to be startled from a nightmare a few minutes later.

In my dream, I am at your apartment when my finger touches accidentally an electric outlet which pulls me in, slowly and persistently, to my death. As the current is not particularly strong, I am initially confident that I can, at will, snatch my finger away, but the pull steadily grows. I try to yank my finger out of the death trap—and find myself woken up all trembling. I am tired. Yours has been the slowest death in the history of the world, and you seem to withstand it far better than I do. I now pray for it to be over. Wishing to find you dead upon arrival. Knowing I won't. I now truly fear that you will not let go of me. Ever.

I dread boarding that plane and entering your web. I am angry. I am neglecting my daughter, leaving my husband to his own devices during the holiday season—damn it—depriving myself of the festivities, the Christmas lights on the Champs-Élysées, the plentiful markets. I voluntarily imprison myself in your dying cave, and all I get in return is contempt and abuse. Not a great bargain.

December 19

I can delay no longer and finally arrive to find you brittle and frail. Too weak to tolerate your artificial teeth that were hurting your gums, your last sign of vanity is now gone, and you look like a caricature of an old witch. Having barely eaten for the past two weeks, you are too lethargic to greet me with the usual fanfare; the twenty-course meal awaiting me on the kitchen table is stored in the drawers of the past and will never be again. You manage to say hello but not even smile. You reach for a white rag from a pile you keep in a drawer by your bed and spit the mucus accumulated in your mouth into it. And when I see your sticks of legs, bones covered by nothing but waxy skin—you, who always had hips and thighs that any Italian mama could have been proud of, cellulite included—these pitiful legs of yours make me want to cry. Your high cheekbones are also covered with parchment-like yellow-ing skin, but when you, with your last drops of feminine pride, hurry to put lipstick on that empty hole of a mouth and then *relax your head against the pillow, I look at you and see the most beautiful woman in the world.*

My "job" so far has not been difficult. Gone is the critical, totalitarian master of the universe who ordered me around or became hysterical. You are mostly peaceful, asking me for a bottle of cold soda, a glass of milk, no more. These you bring slowly, carefully, to your mouth, and I avert my eyes as you drink. Old age is not a pretty sight.

I know that just two months ago, you would have preferred death to your current condition, but you quickly adjust to any new, lower level of existence with an acceptance that astonishes me—just to stay alive, in whatever shape or form.

Yes, part of me was hoping that you would have quietly expired while I was out picking up some fresh bottles of soda or a pack of adult diapers. That this long, long bridge between life and death would have been finally crossed. It is not to be, at least not yet. You are asking for another glass of milk, and I secretly calculate how much longer it could nourish you for. With some shame, I acknowledge that thought, but nevertheless offer you some fresh ice cream or your favorite chocolate to go together with the milk—offers that you, thankfully, decline. I still need you with me, will forever need you. But I am being worn down to the core by this emotional roller coaster, the waiting game that has been going on for years, my constant fear that you will suffer in the process.

I have to call your doctor tomorrow and try to plead with him not to interfere with our chosen path. You are so content in your bed, wrapped in the soft, white, warm covers. I know your horror of hospitals and strangers handling your body. I need to, somehow, get that across to him. The fear of failure, of the doctor doing the "heroic" thing and trying to "save" you, of him being, perhaps, obligated to do so, gnaws at me and keeps me awake this night.

Earlier today, as I left you for a couple of hours, went out of this apartment that has become your private hospital and probable death bed, despite feeling nauseous and your voice barely audible, you parted from me with your habitual, "Drive carefully!"

As you lie dying, you are still instinctively protecting the little girl I am for you. As you lie dying, you are still my mama. That is the part I cannot let go of. Not yet. One more night in my childhood bed, my mama still with me.

December 20–21

*B*eing a "nurse" does not come naturally to me. I woke up at eight o'clock this morning and was summarily summoned by you. You managed to make your way to the kitchen earlier in the day, holding onto the furniture to balance yourself, and were complaining that I had left some unwashed glasses in the sink and the trash had not been taken out. Taking care of those tasks, folding the laundry, getting your drinks, calling the doctor, social services, and the technician to come fix the television, all such minute details took up most of the earlier part of the day and left me drained. You refuse to have anyone sent by social services to help me with your care. I let it be for the time being, preferring not to risk your wrath, but am not sure how long I am able to hold on. I dread the prospect of having to wash your skeletal body and put if off until Thursday. I do not excel at being the dutiful, merciful daughter. Yet, leaving you for a few minutes to get a cup of coffee at the corner café fills me with guilt. More and more I pray for an end.

Two doctors confirmed today that you are in relatively

good shape and will, most likely, carry on for a few weeks or even months. They both remarked on how very much "alive" you are, attached to your existence, how you bask in the love and attention you are getting. Like a baby, an old baby, you are now enjoying the pampering, the comfort, the way your needs are addressed within seconds. You chatted enthusiastically for almost an hour with the Romanian-speaking geriatric specialist I called in, gossiping about the former Romanian royalty and other such nonsense you must have read ages ago in those trashy magazines you used to be addicted to, until I had to leave the room in boredom.

"Your mother will take advantage of this warmth, which she craved and was deprived of all her childhood, to the last minute she possibly can," says Dr. Bergen, throwing some cheap psychological analysis into the bargain.

The diagnosis is good news with a mixed message for me. Because on the practical side, the doctor did not spare me the gruesome details:

"Even though she doesn't eat, your mother may soon start vomiting black bile as the stomach keeps disgorging dead cells and other impurities. Be prepared for that. She'd be enraged to have her spotless white linen soiled."

It means we are not even near the end of this ordeal. It means I may end up hating you before this is all over.

I am tired to the bones. I cannot be angry with you just because I am impatient to be relieved of your burden—but I am. A bit. I do, however, understand your pathetic clinging to life. When the time comes, I will, most likely, do the same.

This evening, for the first in a long time, I can eat, enjoy myself without that rock choking my throat. I can go out without being worried that I will find you dead upon my return. And that is a relief. A great relief. I fall into a comatose sleep.

After barely three hours of restless slumber, I am up again. Still exhausted, but unable to fall back to sleep. I contemplate taking a sleeping pill but don't. I fear not hearing you calling me from the other room. I check on you. Your toothless open mouth is an ugly black hole in the middle of your bony face. You look like a permanent embodiment of Munch's painting The Scream. *A dreadful mask. Why is it so hard for you to die?*

The next day. More administrative arrangements. Going to the bank under your instructions to pay bills and withdraw some cash, I discover that your accounts cannot be touched. You have to either be there personally—which under the current circumstances is a joke—or I should procure a power of attorney, which seems to be a waste of time in light of your imminent death. When a solution finally emerges—you should sign some blank checks that I can later use as needed—my heart sinks as I notice that, in a momentary confusion, or perhaps the beginning of a more serious deterioration, you sign your maiden name. How long has it been since you used that name? Even your first marriage, when you became "Mrs. Weiss," occurred more than sixty-three years ago. And now the template of your initial identity resurfaces from the depths of where it was buried. Your family. Your own parents. Your cozy home. But I, exasperated, have no energy left in me for sentimental musings and impatiently rush you to correct the signature. When you repeat the mistake, I reprimand you for wasting checks—we are down to the last ones.

I console myself in the surprisingly warm December weather. I drive to the boardwalk, enter a bookstore, and armed with reading material, I place myself on the sunny terrace of a restaurant facing the sea. It is not easy to ignore the nagging guilt pouring from every cell of my body. It is time stolen away from you when you have so little left. I am enjoying food while you are starving to death. I am imagining you groaning in bed with nausea while I dip the fried calamari in sauce. By the second drink, the desire for life and pleasure—suppressed during the last few days of eating nothing but oatmeal in identification with your suffering—conquers. I pay and head to a sandwich store to take one out for my dinner, enter a delicatessen to reemerge with two shopping bags full of goodies. That's it for your atoning daughter. The guilt and the indulgence reinforce each other as in a bulimia attack. To quell my conscience, I look for and luckily find a tiny fridge, the size you asked me to buy for you so you can store some cold drinks, your last possible indulgence, just by your bed.

Having bought the fridge, I arrive home triumphant to find you in your usual agony. I notice the anti-nausea pill I left by your bed this morning and hurry to serve it to you. But your swallowing mechanism malfunctions. The pill ends up in the wrong passage, causing a bout of coughing and spitting from your toothless mouth onto the rags you keep in a drawer near the bed—and on me. I weakly tap on your back but, against my will, cannot control my disgust and leave the room, your *desperate efforts to spit up the pill following me. Why does old age have to be so ugly? I am almost angry with you; hell, I am angry with you for clinging so desperately to such a distasteful life. I drop onto the couch in the living room and burst into tears. Had I been able to, I would have killed you myself.*

You manage to regain control over your breathing, and things calm down for a while. You surprise me by accepting my offer to make you a cup of tea. We sip from our respective cups and have a moment of peaceful, loving chat, even laughter. Then you ask me to help you go pee.

The sight of your once juicy, deliciously round behind, now shriveled to just a bit of loose, hanging skin, should not have surprised me considering your weight loss, but it does.

"You are disgusted," you say shyly.

"No," I lie.

When I put you back in your bed, having thrown the soiled underwear into the trash—why bother washing it—you are grateful and apologetic. You are kind and tender in a way that you haven't been in many years. You lie peacefully against your pillows and, as if guessing my wish that it should all be over, you are telling me that you are now the happiest in a long, long time. And I hate myself for wanting to deprive you of this happiness just because I happened to step in the pee you left on the bathroom floor.

Session 18
Quantum Theory
Summer, 2010

Rue Sauval in the early 1980s. We landed, my dorm roommate Roni and I, our two huge backpacks weighing a ton, and found this hotel, eight francs a night, off rue de Rivoli, just steps from the Louvre. It was all very Parisian—the filthy stairwell; flowery, peeling wallpaper; the bedding that may or may not have been washed; and the bidet we had never seen before.

I slept with Pierre, a thirty-something Frenchman who stopped his Citroën when we were hitching a lift on a day trip to the Loire Valley. Pierre bought me my first steak tartare. I had ordered the most expensive steak on the menu and, frankly, was disappointed when the meat arrived raw, looking more like an uncooked hamburger than a juicy steak—but I dutifully ate it all out of sheer embarrassment.

There was Andreas, a cute Italian, with whom I made eye contact near the Centre Pompidou. That continued into a long night, having him join Roni and me in the crummy hotel room, the mattress caving in under the weight of our three bodies. She never forgave me for not waiting until she left the room the next morning to make love to this charming blond. Dominique had the bluest eyes. I couldn't help staring at those eyes and the dirty blond curls when we passed each other on the street, and he subsequently followed me on Boulevard Saint-Germain and struck up a conversation. He made me wash dishes but—the ultimate Parisian—compensated by picking up some pain au chocolat for our breakfast the next morning. Gerard, whom I picked up at Café de la Paix, did not even wait for me to leave before loading the washing machine with the dirty sheets for fear that his wife, vacationing in Spain with the kids, would sense something upon her return. I didn't much care. I was trying to recover from the heartache of a breakup with my law-school boyfriend, and just about *anyone* fit the bill as distraction.

When I had my long tresses cut in a little hair salon across the street from our hotel—where else does one get a fashionable haircut if not in Paris?—I saw a little blond boy with markedly Asian features. I was fascinated. His striking looks, the lovely combination, enchanted me.

"I wish I could have a half-Asian child," I thought.

It couldn't have been further away from a viable possibility at the time.

Fast-forward twenty-eight years. We are crossing the road between the Seine and the Louvre, continuing along rue de Rivoli. It is one o'clock in the morning. As we pass one of the metro airshafts on the street, the stream of air from a passing train below lifts my white summer dress, Marilyn Monroe style, revealing that I don't sport any underwear. Mia and Jane burst out laughing. Mia is delighted to see her fifty-year-old mother behaving as mischievously as a teenager. They are the twenty-two-year-olds now . . . Jane, reddish-blond, could mistakenly be believed to be my daughter. But it is the black-haired Mia and little Elise with the notably half-Asian features who came out of my womb, proving that even the furthest-fetched dreams sometimes do come true. As I follow the footsteps of my younger self through the narrow streets, I trace my story. In reverse.

The weather forecast predicted rain and, indeed, the morning showers threatened to force our little celebration indoors. By noon the sun emerged in between fluffy clouds and dried up the little balcony in the back of the house. The man sent by the caterer was already in full action, turning the couscous-stuffed lamb that was skewered over the pit, making sure it was roasted evenly. The chicken wings emerged from the oven slightly charred, smelling of the pungent teriyaki sauce they had soaked in overnight. And the barely grilled salmon was crispy but moist on the inside. The cherry trees cooperated—as if blessing the event—with plentiful, succulent fruit maturing just at the right time, giving the children among the invitees an opportunity to collect and fill baskets of red rubies. The sounds of laughter, plates being filled, champagne being poured, music, have, for once, been able to deafen even the endless chirping of the birds. I was cruising among the guests offering a refill of champagne, making sure no one was neglected, making introductions—when Jean-Paul, my husband's childhood friend, suddenly took me in his arms and whirled me around in a rock and roll that made my head spin.

Mia flew over from New York, just for a long weekend, to celebrate her mom's fiftieth birthday. Jane, her friend, off from a semester of exchange studies in Madrid, joined her. Perfect bliss. Surrounded by my daughters, husband, many of our closest friends, I bask in the day, ever so grateful for this rare gift bestowed on me by the universe.

The strong beams were slowly turning into slanted rays of light, casting shadows on the old stone walls of the house, on the tall trees stretching to the horizon, and the air was sweet and heavy with the fragrance of midsummer. Only the closest to me, the small group that was the concentrated essence of my life, were still seated around the iron-cast table, sipping chilled white wine, nibbling on leftovers, chatting in more subdued voices. Jean-Marc came over to kiss me good night before turning in, asking, "Please keep the noise level down; the bedroom window is nearby," and we nodded but made no firm commitment.

As the evening turned into night, the moon was hanging low, shining on our small gathering, aided by the little corner lamp, I knew I was right at the peak, the very summit of happiness.

Life at fifty. A perfect milestone for reflection and reevaluation, isn't it? I hesitate to fall into the obvious trap—as if there were a lesson to be learned from the road spread behind, as if I were able to offer some broad, objective view. Even with my inherent arrogance, I am not so vain as to believe that. I am wandering about in this world as blind as a newborn kitten—if anything, less able to decipher my way. The many turns, the choices and accidents of the past have complicated matters to the point of millions of little knots tangled into an incomprehensible mess, impossible to trace back or predict future moves.

Chaos theory—a tiny difference in initial parameters will result in completely different behavior of a complex system, rendering long-term prediction impossible. Had I not left home at twenty-six with an open ticket to the moon. Had I not worked at that store in Queens for five dollars an hour to support my bar review course. Had I gone to a different restaurant with the one-time date I met at the singles get-together organized by the synagogue on the Upper West Side and missed overhearing the noisy redneck sitting next to me at the counter telling his girlfriend about these really cheap flights to Tokyo. Had the ticket not been so surprisingly reasonable. Had the telephone line not been busy when my Japanese host tried to call and set me up with a young man, a promising member of the upper class. Had I been ordered by the mama-san to sit at a different table while hostessing at the Rabbit Eye Karaoke Club. Had I not met the drunken young Japanese businessman who came in. Had he gone to a different club with his colleagues. Had he not tried to grab my breasts while we were singing, "I Left My Heart in San Francisco" together—the only song I could somehow mumble—and later become the father of my daughters. Had I decided to adhere to the pleas of that tall, handsome, Jewish accountant I'd met just a few days before heading to Japan and taken the flight back to New York instead of getting married in a Shinto ceremony to a complete stranger. And, twenty years later, had I been patient enough to wait for the relationship with Ben to work out (perhaps it did—in a parallel universe). Had I chosen the resort in Portugal instead of the one in Corsica—or even the other one (on the other side of the bay) *in* Corsica—it could have probably ended with no particular consequences just like any "normal" vacation. I'd still be in my suburban house, planning to "someday visit Paris . . ." So many "what ifs." Which one was a missed opportunity and which a lucky turn of events? So many seemingly random occurrences, each a crossroad leading to a whole different life. When I walked into that travel agency to buy my first plane ticket to run away from you, so far away from you—I didn't know any of this.

How does one program randomness?

Was I a particle in a quantum theory model, being statistically hit by other randomly flying objects and stirred aimlessly in various directions? Even as secular a mind as mine has difficulties wrapping itself around that possibility. We would like to see a purpose to this life, a pattern, a moral. Being the confirmed atheist that I am, I do not see a goal— but I do see a path that was imposed by my endowment, an inability to say "no" to adventure, a curiosity, a need to taste every flavor life has to offer. And a response to the fears and traumas you endured but were tattooed in my skin. My life being an effort to address, amend, remedy, reverse, and forget those experiences you planted in me. Epigenetics—the inheritance of memories.

Indeed, I could have met different people along the way and ended up in different places. But I would have always been out there in the field playing the game. I would not have been able to opt for the more secure sidelines, a safer and more tranquil existence. I could not have been able to live my life differently. The choices were far more limited than one would have liked to believe.

Life at fifty. As predictable in its haphazard ways as programmed randomness. A bitterly delicious paradox.

The party is over now. Everyone, including my nocturnal daughters, is retired to bed. We are all safe—temporarily, but at least under the same roof. I have brought us thus far and, like God on the seventh day of creation, I am pleased with what I have accomplished.

Session 19
Farewells

A ct II. The following scenes are a string of "farewells." I move further back into the past and unveil layer after layer, an onion of farewells. I dig deeper and find each tier marked by the one preceding it. By our fifties we must have learned the art of farewells. We kick and refuse to part; like two-year-olds, we cling to the life we know. Finally, we do—fearfully, but nevertheless, accept; sulking, but finally embrace. Because at fifty, one knows that, just like the "creative destruction" economists tell us about, there are farewells we *need* in order to move on; they threaten to tear us apart but eventually propel us on. And, sooner or later, there are very few that one doesn't recover from.

Farewells to homes (and mere houses), lovers (and mere boyfriends or one-night stands), best friends (and ad hoc ones), father, sister (and just family), jobs, colleagues, cats and dogs, teachers, old pianos, hopes. Each leaving a scar, shallow or deep.

Farewell to my daughters' childhood. Waving them—the

two babies I had held up to that moment under my wings, the two young women they have become—on to their own journey. I follow their footsteps and, with a gentle pat on their well-pampered behinds, I encourage them, at my own peril, to take a solo flight out of the nest. Many such flights are to follow, each increasing in distance, and as time inevitably passes, their absences will stretch longer than their home-comings. I wave to them, a brave smile plastered on my face. When did I, the carefree twenty-six-year-old happily waving goodbye to her own mother on her way to conquer the world, turn into this middle-aged, battle-scarred *woman*? When did I sign up to play the "mother" role in this mini-drama?

At fifty, we are on top of the game. Some of our more glorious battles are behind us, and we are now more confident in our ability to take on those heading our way. That is when the angel of death lazily picks up his scythe and has the last laugh.

Part III

REGRETS

Session 20
The Cuckoo's Nest
Normandy, Summer 2011

After the meal and a delicious nap, a walk through the fields, continuing down a narrow path in the shade of the lush forest, circling back to the deserted village, its houses fainting in the afternoon heat. A light breeze wipes the sweat off our foreheads. A lone tractor toils on the horizon, biting into the ground.

The heavy, dark smell of earth—so different from the thin, dusty Israeli soil—is oddly familiar, conjuring some atavistic memories. The woods smell like forbidden Christmas trees. My tiny feet, clad in ankle-high white leather shoes have stomped on this terrain. I hear the cows of my childhood mooing in the distance; the scent of their manure kisses my nostrils like an old acquaintance. The velvety raw milk I buy from the next-door farmer tastes like theirs, when I drank it straight from the milkmaid's container. The train tracks seem to stretch all the way from Transylvania; that little chugging steam locomotive that once almost ran me down as I was crossing the rails, hurrying to my mom's calling, should be passing by soon. These are the plums from which my great-grandfather used to produce *palinka*. The trees are heavily laden with those long-ago berries. The Gypsies must be hiding up in the hills. My ghosts are surrounding me, dancing an inviting Hungarian *czardas*.

"We missed you," they say. "Welcome home."

"It is nice to be back," I reply.

It seems like an eternity since I first sat on these very steps leading down from the house to its vast property. Brick steps, somewhat crooked, peppered with moss. The treetops were tickling the sky on the horizon—just as they do now—with nothing but apple and pear trees in between. I was here for a few stolen days on the heels of a London business trip, scouting out law firms for our next megadeal. For Jean-Marc and me, it was our first live encounter since we met in Corsica, our one night in Paris, and the endless emails that followed. I took the Eurostar from Waterloo station, still wearing my black tweed business suit, partially to impress him. He waited at Gare du Nord and after a quickie and a visit to a Gauguin exhibition, I was practically pushed into the Volvo and whisked off to Normandy.

His country house was impressive, if rundown and unkempt, cobwebs everywhere. Completely isolated, the green pastures stretched all the way to the fences in the distance. It was picturesque on the border of being kitsch—wooden beams and all; there was even a well—without ever falling into the trap.

We went to the local market to shop for the most succulent blood sausages curled into long, thick ropes, with the vendor cutting off just the length I requested; the deepest smelling, ripest, heart-shaped cheeses; the freshest eggs—the yolks a smooth, dark yellow begging to be swallowed raw. I prepared little meals that I served him in front of the television while he watched a rugby game. We were living a romantic movie. An escape from reality. At least from *my* reality—all this was so obvious for *him*.

"Too bad I am leaving tomorrow," I told Jean-Marc as he kissed me, holding me tight in his embrace,

"I don't want to think about it," he replied.

His loneliness was as thick as a heavy odor in the air between us, threatening, in an instant, to suck me into its bottomless depth. And I told myself, "You'd better escape right now. There will be no way back."

But that thought was soon forgotten, swept away in the autumn wind together with the blood-red leaves.

On the last day of my mini-vacation, I tried to forget about my boss, the business calls I had been avoiding, and just enjoy those precious moments of serenity. I tried to de-stress. But Elise, missing me on the other end of the line, was tugging at my heart. We "belly button charged" —our ritual of connecting from a distance, holding our respective belly buttons while on the phone—as if "recharging" our love, but that did not alleviate my guilt. I sat on the steps, surrounded by tranquility, drowning in the green beauty of Normandy, the silence, a cock crowing in the distance, a cow mooing, nothing else.

As I soaked up as much as I possibly could of the calm, I felt my eyes fill up with tears. I was crying for myself. For my life, in which such peace was nothing but a passing, fleeting moment before I returned to the forty-second floor of my midtown office building with its constant "deals," the investment jargon that I could barely, though I pretended to, understand. The yields, basis points, bonuses, gross-up clauses, my fingernails bleeding, digging into the corporate mud, in an effort to hold on to my job with one hand—while drafting checks, the mortgage payments, the car lease with the other, sitting at the kitchen table writing thousands of dollars away, paying the gardener, the nanny, the cleaning lady—full salaries for multiple people—and, yes, almost forgot, battling with a rebellious teenager and keeping up a cheerful demeanor for my six-year-old. That moment of fresh air, that passing image of a very different life, hurt. The contrast was too sharp. I looked around, and it was a fine picture of a life that was not mine. The following day, I kissed Jean-Marc goodbye and got on the plane.

And I didn't know that some years later, as the long day folded into a dark blue light, I would be sitting on the same steps. An almost full moon would be shining and the treetops starting to cast dim shadows on the horizon. I would ask Jean-Marc whether the little antique lamp in the corner of the house worked, and instead of answering he would just turn it on. A magical light would flood the round iron outdoor table and chairs that used to be on the wooden deck in our New York house and are now placed on the stone deck in this remotest of little French villages. I didn't know.

The house behind me is now beautifully renovated and updated with the newest appliances. The grounds haven't changed, though. They hold the same enchanting beauty, tranquility, silence. The only apparent danger is branches of roses shooting their thorny hands to catch onto my bare skin and leave a thin trail of blood as a souvenir. The investment banking lingo is fading in the back of my mind with few regrets. Elise is doing her homework in what is now "Elise's room." I go to the market or to the small shops in the next little town where most of the vendors recognize me by now as "the American" and greet me with a friendly welcome. All those worries and the constant sense of running just to keep in place are gone. The fleeting moment turned into a life.

And I try to remember my younger self, the woman who sat right here for a moment of repose, a stolen temporary bliss. Had she known then where it would lead to, that an improvised quickie following a business trip would end up causing her to exchange independence for serenity. Had she been given the full picture—what would she have chosen? How could the struggling single mother have judged a life that was then so far away? Alas, I can no longer see into her thoughts or communicate with her. That life faded too far into memory to be re-felt. The river had flowed on, and that woman drifted away with it.

I still try to capture that instant of peace. It is not easy. Life has changed, but I have not. I am still on guard, always on my toes. I am still restless and feel as much in constant danger. For me, there will always be other landscapes, other

smells, other longings. I sometimes miss the bitter aroma of
Arab coffee with cardamom; the coffee of my student days,
drunk in the narrow alleys of the old market in Jerusalem.
Other times, the smell of soy sauce rising from the stalls selling *takoyaki*, octopus balls, during summer festivals in Tokyo.
And all the while, my feet feel like erupting in an intoxicating
dance of *czardas* played on the radio. I miss the places I have
known and the places I have not, the places I have been to and
the places I have yet to go.

I am a guest performer in this play of a peaceful Normandy
existence. Unlike the waitress in the café where we sat this
morning, unlike each of the farmers who present their merchandise at the market, unlike the neighbor who runs a farm
and a rural bed and breakfast, unlike Jean-Marc. Each of
them, like the trees and the river, belongs to this landscape.
I am but a stand-in, executing the part, redecorating rooms,
placing the chicken in the oven, picking cherries, making jam
and sherry brandy, all the while wondering whether I will get
to drink it. Planting seeds in the little space by the outdoor
dining area, skeptical about my chances of seeing them grow.
With the tradition of making liquor that I must have inherited intuitively from my great-grandfather—burying plums
in vodka bottles—I have also inherited the memory of burying oneself in the barrel, hiding from yesterday's drinking
buddy. I do it well, but I am, nevertheless, a fake. No matter
how many husbands with gentile last names I collect, I don't
belong and never will. The place I belonged to had gone up in
smoke even before I was born. My roots are airborne—they

cannot thrive in this soil. I am paralyzed with fear. This home is but a trap.

Like you—and it was my own doing—I ended up alone. A stranger who does not even speak the language. I am still and will always be your daughter. The phenomenal fruit of a burnt tree. How long will I be sitting on these steps? I don't know the answer. I do know that neither Jean-Marc nor any of the others ever asks themselves such questions.

Last night I saw the shadowy silhouette of a bat flying in circles. It was the first time in my life I had seen a bat.

Session 21
My Glass of Wine
Anywhere, Always

M y glass of wine and I have sat together in lots of places. It has been, by far, my most faithful of companions. To be precise, it isn't always wine. Sometimes it's a cosmo or another cocktail containing more than a fair amount of vodka. It is rarely champagne. Champagne is to rejoice, to celebrate. When I sit alone with my glass of whatever it is, it is never to celebrate. Loneliness is not to be celebrated. Loneliness is to be initially savored, with a false sense of control. The first glass is followed by a second while nibbling on nuts or olives, whichever is being offered. I am examining from the corner of my eye the fellow passengers. I ignore the couples. I size up the women sitting alone, but those are few, if any—usually none but me. I focus on the men. They, in turn, examine me. I am the new merchandise. I absentmindedly read a few pages of my book. There is always a book to serve as my companion. It is a Holy Trinity: the glass, the book, me. The book is a barrier or an opening, whichever I choose it to be. I hide behind it, block access, use it as a shield or else as a trap to commence a conversation.

"What are you reading?"

The common banal initiation, with whichever random soul I choose to share my loneliness for a few minutes or a night.

My glass of—let's say, wine—never disappoints or betrays me. By the third, the control gives way to a slow drowning. The pace picks up, and the glass is emptied faster. I no longer sip—I drink. I am still in control, but I am the captain at the helm of a sinking ship. The book loses its barrier option and is tossed aside. Oblivion is the only remaining possibility.

Occasionally, I used to find myself in "situations." Like the time loneliness drove me into the city at ten o'clock on a Saturday night. It was raining cats and dogs, the heavy drops pouring on the roof of my beautiful Jaguar, the windshield wipers dancing at a maniacal pace. Blinded by the curtain of water, I drove on nevertheless, pushed relentlessly ahead by a force stronger than me. But that is just a form of expression because truth is, the force *was* me, it was the essence of me. I needed to feel people, even complete strangers, around me, to confirm my existence in the mirror of their eyes. So despite the rain—or because of the rain—I drove myself all the way downtown to Mercer Street, just south of Houston. It was rather simple to find parking on a night such as that, and I landed in a cozy but very chic restaurant. I was seated in the one vacant spot left at the bar, next to a very tall, good-looking man. He was good-looking in an unusual way, a bit bizarre, his hair and complexion very fair, almost albino, awkward in his movements as if he were not yet used to his height. I ordered my drink and some fabulous olives, spread my book in front of me, and warmed up in the glow of the casually elegant clientele. Many seemed to know each other, kissing and greeting their arriving friends to the sound of clinking glasses, forks and knives in action, *oohs* and *aahs* over the simple yet exquisite food.

And the man alone at the bar. My internal radar zoomed in and started sending out wordless signals—a stolen but obvious glance, a flutter of eyelashes, a noticeably self-conscious rearrangement of that errant curl. He was too experienced to miss them. He started a conversation: the food, the reputation of the place, what he was doing in New York, what he did in general (CEO, what else?). A few words about me—I was creating whatever role I intended to play for the evening. It didn't take long to feel as if we had known each other forever. I have always had a gift for creating that kind of instant intimacy with men. At that point, I was barely able to drive him to his exclusive hotel, where we took the elevator upstairs together, and it was clear that I was going to stay the night. As we kissed and he started feeling my body—acting more out of obligation than passion—I asked him in a teasing voice, "Would you prefer sleeping with me now and never see me again, or would you rather we just cuddle and continue seeing each other?"

"Are those the only two options?" He smiled.

"Yes," I confirmed with an equally challenging lightness.

He was British and well brought up, the product of elite schools, proper manners, and accent. He had no choice but to be polite, so the answer was the obvious. It may also be that he had to catch an early flight, was tired, and rather relieved not to have to bother with the messy act. We slept in each other's arms, fully clothed. And we parted the next morning with the knowledge that we had each met our soul mate. We exchange several emails the following days and weeks. We planned to meet on my next visit to London. But then, somehow, things lapsed, and when I ended up calling him many years later while on a business trip to the UK, his secretary told me he was by then living in Dubai, and that was that.

That is a story I do like to remember. There is a bittersweet melancholy to it. A promise of a romance, even if missed—it could have ended as a fairy tale, though it didn't. I fondly hold to that memory and am grateful to my little glass.

Other stories—such as the one that started with a similarly innocent glass of wine at a singles party but ended in the emergency room of the Greenwich, Connecticut, hospital—I would rather forget. Another stranger, a good Samaritan—this time I am unable to remember his face—found me on a bench at the last stop of the wrong train and must have driven me to the emergency room. I woke up to find I had lost my watch, coat, and one shoe of a pair that I loved, and faced a stern scolding from the tired doctor whose nightshift I had invaded.

Your reaction to this second, less romantic story was, nevertheless, revealing. Of course, I told you. I tell you everything. There are no secrets, no barriers between us. Instead of a reprimand, you took it calmly, as if the relief of knowing

I ended up relatively safe erased any possible anger. Without any need for explanations, you understood instinctively how the stress of holding it all together, the responsibility for the kids, house, work could compel me to seek such a destructive release. There was no prudish criticism coming from your end, just matter-of-fact compassion.

"You got it out of your system," you said. "This should suffice for a couple of years. There is no harm in letting it all go every now and then. But be careful."

And no more. I was a million pounds lighter. In two sentences, you had released me from the regret, the guilt, the shame. As if with a magic wand, you had healed me and moved on to the next topic.

Many years have gone by. The loneliness now resides in a more-or-less stable marriage. I am more than six thousand miles away from that downtown restaurant, as well as the Greenwich Hospital in Connecticut. Random nights in strangers' or hospital beds are but a distant memory. So why am I still sitting in a deserted café in rural Normandy, nursing my sadness with a book and a glass of, well, this time Kir? The loneliness, I couldn't change. The bartender and the local truck drivers are sending not-so-subtle glances toward me, a woman, so obviously an outsider, so obviously sad. This is familiar and comforting. So are the tears finally returning to my eyes.

Was it really just a few years ago that I was taking a moment of repose from the rat race of corporate America?

That I was trying to forget my world, a world in which one has to respond within a second to each email received on the closely watched, always attached BlackBerry? The pressed clients scrambling in fear of being left behind, of losing a moment's opportunity to make their bonuses. I was just an overnight guest, basking in this island of calm, unable to even imagine it for myself. In the interim, the world turned over a couple of times, I waved goodbye to those rough American shores, joined Jean-Marc in his "old world," sharing his life, his weekends in the country, long Sunday lunches followed by him smoking a cigar while I . . .

While I what? The BlackBerry has, indeed, quieted almost to a silence. It was replaced by newer devices, equipped for fun applications rather than work. But I still check my messages every few minutes, this time in search of a signal that could pierce my idle existence, bring a fresh breeze of change, extract me from what became so quickly—so subtly that I didn't even notice—an asylum. The door is open, but I can no longer fly. I flap my wings in vain. I am tamed now. Here, in the land of black-and-white spotted cows, food and drink are abundant, but always measured carefully in self-imposed equilibrium. And when I rebel with my usual excesses, such vulgar indulgences are commented on in the name of love. Little ingenuous remarks such as, "Are you *still* eating?" followed by a grimace of thinly veiled disgust. A snide look as I don't fit into pants that used to be comfortable.

How could such bile of bitterness build up so quickly between two people who just recently made passionate love but grew too close for comfort? How easily an insensitive comment—well placed to subtly prick—could become an insult? A hurt from which the relationship may perhaps resurrect itself, but be maimed, the spearheads buried just below skin level, sending painful, periodic reminders. The age of innocence is over.

And you? You still feel me without words. You sense my discontent. This time there is no quiet compassion. This time I am in for severe scolding and "instructions" to hang onto my marriage, be accepting, a "good wife." Of course, you don't believe what you are preaching, but you are, again, trying desperately to protect me. My marital discontent scares you far more than any drunken episodes ever did. You now fear I can no longer stand on my own feet, you have lost confidence in my ability to fend for myself, you think I would be helpless without these crutches. I tell myself that you only reflect on me your own insecurities. I tell myself these worries are the phantoms of an old, feeble mind. And I fiercely argue, our conversations often ending with me hanging up on you in fury. But the truth is that without you to instill confidence in me, I am not quite so sure. I argue my case, trying to convey independence, to convince myself as well as you—but the spark is gone. I am paralyzed, letting my feet be planted further and further, sinking deeper and deeper into the heavy Normandy soil, growing hideous roots, buried, until I am not at all sure I can lift them anymore.

My husband, in his now habitual manner, berates me for this and that. He gets all agitated and waves his hands about. His handsome features become distorted. I sit and watch the man I loved turn into a raging foe. I sit and watch him hating me.

How did we get to this so quickly? What is this battle about? It never is about anything. It is always about us. Being trapped in the other. A woman, lonely and sad, yes, but independent and free. The one who could drink until she dropped off her bar stool now sharing a demure half-bottle of wine with an equilibrated husband. The man who was looking for a quiet retirement, a bit of excitement here and there but not too much, panicking at the sight of his hard-earned savings dwindling, being consumed by this irrational spendthrift. It's about our habits and insecurities. It's about building cages around those whose free spirit we used to admire. It's about wanting protection but being suffocated by it. The love is still there, hidden among the rubble, but as with an earthquake, not all survivors can be actually rescued.

It's not that hard to go to the other room, pat him on the head, give him a light kiss, say, "But I still love you—let's stop this madness."

He would be as relieved as I. And, in all honesty, I could just as easily, in a different mood, describe this "cage" as a comfortable nest to settle cozily into and doze off. A warm existence of two souls who are not always compatible but know there are no alternatives. After all, how long can one constantly fly? I have circled this earth time and again. Perhaps it is possible to rest on this branch for more than just the night. Perhaps it was possible. If we could only abandon this war. If only we could.

I don't walk up the corridor to his room. I am too tired. This meaningless war has gone too far. He made one too many nasty remarks for me to forget. The rage on his face was more pronounced this time. I am paralyzed with fatigue; the pointless little, spiteful battles have zapped away my energy and strength. I am only able to collapse in another room, another bed, alone. We each lick our wounds in our respective corners, comfort ourselves with the same old lies we are used to telling ourselves, crawl deeper inside, and disconnect. Battery discharged.

Session 22

The Fading Pulse of the Umbilical Cord

When I brought you home—wheeled you from the hospital bed to the rental car and practically carried you up the stairs to your apartment—you were a broken rag of a woman. With an aching heart, I left you with a young Romanian caregiver I hurriedly found with the help of a relative, not sure whether or not she understood the complicated schedule in which the dozens of pills had to be administered. Not sure whether I'd ever see you again. I returned to my own home, duties, and daughter, a tear-soaked shadow of myself.

The Romanian aide was thrown out within three days. The bottles of medication followed suit a day or two later. Within a week you'd pulled yourself up by your hair and started cleaning. Within a month you were back on your feet. You were making rounds at the neighborhood shops, telling everyone who'd listen that you'd invented an ultimate remedy for cancer—tea with lemon. Had the self-important

head of the oncology department who predicted your imminent death crossed your path, he would have had to take shelter from you speeding past him on the electric scooter you
bought. Soon, the only manifestation of the cancer that so
shocked us when first discovered was the constant mindset
of "I am a sick and lonely woman" you adopted. Who can
blame you? How would I have reacted to having such a sword
hanging over my head?

Time has passed, and the sword did not drop. Far from it.
You thrived. With time being a depleting commodity, your
attachment to life only grew. When you felt as if another
blood clot was on its way to clog your arteries, you stubbornly
dragged yourself out of bed and, holding on to the furniture,
kept walking around the apartment all night long to maintain
the blood flow. You claimed you hardly ate, yet your weight
showed no sign of dropping. You used industrial quantities
of suppositories and seemed to take pleasure in telling me
the details of your bowel movements. You became an expert
rider, naming your scooter "my motorcycle," visiting this or
that store, taking care of light shopping. The heavier stuff—
groceries, vegetables—was ordered and delivered to you by
shop owners who were more than willing to oblige, charmed
by the sweet grandma they saw in you. Even your limited
vocabulary in Hebrew was turned to an advantage, an additional weakness everyone was eager to help you with. You are
in better shape than ever. And so is your madness.

And I haven't "talked" to you in a long while, at least not
in this form of a monologue that you would never read. Our

actual conversations during this time have been strained, at
best. I could not handle your constant accusations and complaints of loneliness, as if Monika's rejection of you were somehow my fault, as if we were accomplices in the same crime. I
became fed up with trying to please you and never being able
to come even close. My telephonic greetings on your birthday
were summarily dismissed. No flowers were accepted. They
all reminded you of your loneliness, as if I had offered them
as a "consolation prize" for not being there.

When I came for a visit, it usually ended up with you sulking for one reason or another. In the lovely Scottish Hotel in
Tiberius, you went on a hunger strike. I can't recall the cause
of the minor argument we had had the previous evening, but
it resulted in your sitting at the breakfast buffet—the tables
laden with multiple kinds of bread, an endless assortment of
cheeses, yogurts, cold cuts, herrings, salads, fruit, and home-
made jams—purposely taking no notice of one of the most
impressive spreads I have ever seen, drinking plain coffee
with an insulted look plastered onto your face. The more I
begged you to eat, the more stubborn you became.

The same scene repeated itself when I flew you over to
France for a visit. A comment about the transparency of
your skirt cost me hundreds of euros wasted on a dinner at a
Michelin-starred restaurant. You wouldn't grace the delicacies you were served with a single glance. The ensuing tour
of the Champagne region, which I had planned thinking that
the landscape—peppered with grapevines and picturesque
farmhouses—would remind you of your childhood, left you

unimpressed. You waited until we were dozens of miles away from Paris to let me know that you would have preferred to stay in the city and spend our time window-shopping.

Your faithful girlfriends did not fare better. They were the ones sustaining you with a visit and warm soup throughout the flu you caught every winter, accompanying you to hospitals for this test or that because you couldn't handle the maze of administration with your very limited Hebrew. One day you were telling me Magda was the kindest, spending days with you going from one clinic to another, only to find out that she had become your bitter enemy the following day.

"I don't ever want to hear her name mentioned," you shouted over the phone.

Edith was your best friend on that long journey from one concentration camp to the next. As young brides, you shared a backyard—cooking together, gossiping together, pregnant together. Until one day she, too, offended you somehow. I stopped following the twists and turns of your convoluted mind, ravaged by loneliness and malady.

"Don't ever trust any girlfriends," your poisonous voice regularly whispered in my ears.

Meanwhile, that tiny circle of old women was all you had to rely on for support.

During holidays—Jewish New Year, Passover, and even minor ones, such as Chanukah or Purim—you sensed your solitude even more acutely. I made it to one Seder night, taking time off from work (vacations in corporate America or French banks did not exactly correspond to the Jewish holiday calendar). I arrived in Tel Aviv for forty-eight hours, landing at midnight. But how often can one pull that off? How could I juggle between spending holidays with my daughters and your needs, which always took precedence?

Nor do I have to delve too far into my subconscious to admit that I did not much feel like taking these compulsory trips to your crazily decorated apartment, being stuffed with heavy Hungarian food, then driving you around with no real purpose other than taking advantage of the rental car to satisfy your desire to get out of the house. You never tired of it. I have no doubt that you were the only eighty-something-year-old doing the rounds to find out which restaurants were open past midnight and ordering steak and chips at two in the morning at the Brasserie. Any attempts to see friends my age turned into guilt trips: "How can you leave me alone when you are here for such a short time?"

My culpability only reinforced by the truth of your accusations, I ended up being hostage to your demands. So, yes, I tried to avoid those trips. Much easier to spend a week in the French Alps where my only care in the world was not falling off my skis. Even on one of the numerous occasions that you were hospitalized—when a neighbor made the overseas telephone call to inform me of the news—I did not interrupt my purchase of a splendid pair of Sonia Rykiel shoes after I hung up. And, yes, I felt bad—but not enough to renounce my pleasures. You spent your birthday, yet again, alone.

Those extravagant shoes ended up being useful, nevertheless. Knowing your quest for beauty, I brought them over in my suitcase, yet unworn, on one of my following visits. You were gravely ill on that occasion and bedridden, each inhalation a struggle followed by severe coughing. Yet, you spared no energy in carefully examining the intricate design and then asked me to place them near you—on your spotless, white sheets—so you had the gratification of glancing at such work of art whenever you opened your eyes. Some things don't change.

I woke up in the early morning hours and, for some unknown reason, started talking to you again, in my head. It happened at other times as well, but I never acted upon it. This time the words formed in my mind, forcing their way out, and my fingers were typing them automatically on an imaginary keyboard. I nevertheless willed myself to wait. As if to test the desire—is it compelling enough or just a momentary whim?

I prepared the beans that are going to accompany the main course at lunch. It's end-of-February weather outside. Perfect for a hearty dish of duck and beans. I peeled almost three heads of garlic, browned them lightly in goose fat, added onion, bacon, seasoning, and the beans that have been soaking all night. Poured enough boiling water to cover all the ingredients in the pot.

Cooking is one of the only "neutral" subjects that you and I can still talk about without getting into a fight. I know immediately what mood you are in according to how condescending you are at my description, over the phone, of what I am making for lunch or dinner. If you are in a foul mood, the soup I am preparing resembles "wash water." On more cheerful occasions, I fare somewhat better. There are some domains of which you are less possessive, on which your judgment is not as harsh, but with respect to those that are marked as *your* territory—cooking, cleaning, being beautiful—in short, being a *woman*—you are not sharing the glory.

As a child, I was not allowed to set foot in the kitchen. I was designated for more "intellectual" pursuits to which, rightly or wrongly, you did not have any claims—hence I did not "compete" with you. Yet, even if the gift did not manifest itself for the longest time, I did eventually inherit your passion for cooking. My cuisine is about creativity and innovation, new combinations and textures. Yours, not only old-fashioned Hungarian, but specifically Transylvanian.

"They," you say, meaning Hungarians, "cook differently than we do."

There was no need asking who did a better job at that.

As a child, I was neither a good nor an adventurous eater. You had to tell me stories, press buttons on my nose, fly airplanes in order to get that fork laden with the eternal chicken cutlet and puree, my favorite dish, into my unwilling mouth.

All that is in the distant past. Now I search for exotic delicacies, have eaten crickets in the markets of Beijing and slurped live baby octopus in Seoul. That childlike curiosity, the fearlessness of trying anything new—that too I inherited from you. I still recall you devouring with your eyes and tasting without hesitation some mussels at the gourmet grocer's I took you to in Manhattan. You were about seventy years old, and those were your first mussels. Unlike most people, who by that age are set in their ways, you enthusiastically opened your eyes, mouth, senses, and mind to novelty.

Today's traditional-French-lunch-with-a-twist is on its way. The beans are simmering slowly on the stove, the duck thighs are coated in a marinade of honey, olive oil, salt, pepper, and soy sauce, waiting to be deposited in the oven. There are some last-minute preparations to be concluded— setting the table, chopping and adding the fresh herbs. I leave those for later. I am anxious, as if we had a secret rendezvous, to join you here on these pages. To put down all that has been written in my mind during those early morning hours. To bridge the last year. And to continue this process of severing the umbilical cord. Or am I just tying it even tighter?

When Elise, my youngest, was little, I told her that we were forever connected by an invisible umbilical cord. Having nursed her for over two years, I had to tear her off my breasts when I was forced by the economic reality of the divorce to go back to work. Perhaps it was time. There were few, but nevertheless some, business trips where I had to stay overnight. Later, years later, when I met Jean-Marc, there were a few more days stolen on the tail end of such a trip. Elise's voice over the phone, too far away. Before each departure, we would lie on my bed with our belly buttons touching and "charge" the connection between us, as if it were a battery. We called it a "belly button charge." We stayed in that position for as long as it took, depending on the length of the trip, until Elise announced finally, "It's fully charged."

Then we felt ready for the separation. When it was too long for one charge to suffice, we would do it remotely. We would each put a finger to our respective belly buttons and hold it there while on the phone until her voice on the other end of the line determined, "It's fully charged."

That invisible umbilical cord stretched with endless flexibility—across oceans and faraway continents.

My umbilical cord remained attached to you throughout our twenty-five years apart. From that day, when you escorted me, with my two suitcases, to the airport. It extended to a tiny doll-house-like apartment in a sinful and decadent Tokyo, back to New York. It was nourishing me with support in a posh New York suburb and now in elegant Paris. It stretched life spans from the communist Romania of my childhood and from the ultra-Orthodox religious neighborhood I grew up in near Tel Aviv. Throughout that entire voyage, our umbilical connection was neither imaginary nor invisible. It was stronger than the elements, the laws of physics, distances, malady, even periods of extreme anger and long silences. That same umbilical cord is still strapped around my neck. With you, your heavy weight hanging on it, clinging to life. And I hold to it, on my end, as if my life depended on it as well.

Session 23

Visits to the Mad House

Suburbs of Tel Aviv, April 2013

Passover. You were still well enough, but I felt it might be your last. You complained endlessly about being lonely during the holidays, trying to shut your ears to the chanting from the many synagogues nearby. The noise of dishes being cleared from tables and replaced by fresh ones reached you through the walls from the neighboring apartments that were inhabited by large Orthodox Jewish families and filled your heart with envy. You declined invitations from your friends and preferred to stay home alone, jealous of their merriment, of the presence of their grandchildren chasing each other from room to room. You stayed home and turned the television on high volume. And your sulking voice made me pay for every moment of absence.

I thought bringing your granddaughters over for Passover would please you. I thought that sharing a Seder night with you, having a rare opportunity to feast on your heavy Hungarian dishes—which represent our "home cooking"— would be a precious, lasting memory for them.

Excitedly, we knocked on your door. You opened—and the "madness show" started. Without a greeting, you banged the bowls of food on the table, more than twenty different dishes materialized, appeared, and were removed with nervous energy before we had a chance to taste them, then were quickly discarded into the trash in front of our disbelieving eyes. You never sat on a chair to join us. When we tried to pour a bit of holiday spirit into the chaotic food parade and sing a few holiday songs, you got so enraged that, eclipsing our voices, you shouted over and over again, "This is *not* a holiday for me!"

Confused, shocked, and disappointed, the girls moved uneasily in their chairs while I was mortified by the horror of the display you put up for them to witness. An undying memory of a holiday with their dying—but perhaps not fast enough—grandma.

My heart sank lower and lower in despair as your gestures, agitation, hysteria whirled around, threatening to carry us with you into your own private madhouse. Finally, Elise could take it no longer and burst into a hilarious laughter, which infuriated you even further. But she had shown us a way out. Ignoring you, we continued singing the holiday songs in exaggerated comic accents, creating our own joke, releasing the heavy weight of tension with a more positive lunacy. We kept at it, erecting a wall of hilarity as our defense, singing louder and louder, the folly becoming sillier and more absurd.

As soon as you realized that you had lost your evil hold on

us—that we had managed to escape your spell—the demon that had taken hold of you was defeated. You calmed down, by now a bit embarrassed, and the rest of the evening was almost pleasant. The girls, forever compassionate, sensed the deep anxiety that had provoked such a primal reaction in you, that helpless panic that had moved you to insanity. Rather than resentful, they felt sorry for you. By midnight they were seated beside you, each tucked under one of your arms. Your hands, pleasantly rough after all those years of using cleaning detergents, were rhythmically caressing their soft virginal skin as you hummed the kitschy tune from the movie *Casablanca*—"As Time Goes By"—moving Elise to tears. Like tender chicks gathering under your wings for warmth, the girls basked in this pittance of rare grandmotherly love.

But I swore to myself, "Never again."

And, indeed, it never would be again. When we parted from you, waving to the silhouette of the fragile old woman standing on the pavement becoming smaller and smaller as the car pulled away, Mia was crying, knowing she would never see you again.

You turned back, trying to walk up the hill leading to your apartment building, to your lonely existence, and—as the neighbors later told me—collapsed in tears midway. They rushed to your aid, carrying you up the stairs and into your perfectly arranged and spotlessly clean "museum" of an apartment, where only the noise of the television and the ringing of my daily telephone calls would pierce the silence. You have long regretted those hated, uncontrollable outbursts, wishing you could erase them; you would be crying inconsolably for days to get over the missed opportunity for happiness. This and many others.

The next day, making a final tour along Tel Aviv's main boulevard, Dizengoff Street, we stopped at a café restaurant serving traditional Jewish cuisine. The girls couldn't help themselves from ordering a few dishes as a farewell to the food they so rarely get to eat. When the chicken soup with lukewarm matzo balls and the tasteless pickled tongue arrived, Elise lamented mournfully, "We could have had far better ones at Grandma's."

Yes, we could have had. But no—we couldn't have.

And all three of us averted our eyes in embarrassment when our car sped along the highway on our way to the airport, passing your apartment building without stopping.

I went alone on the next visit. The same drill. Months of pent-up loneliness bursting into endless demands to be taken to restaurants, cafés, shops, movies—a bottomless well of needs. I obliged. Woken up by you standing over my bed, all dressed up and ready to go at seven o'clock in the morning, I tried to please you but, predictably, to no avail. As your legs started failing, you asked to be driven around for hours on end. Rains of bitterness were pouring down on my head—your ceaseless, nonsensical conversation a constant background noise I could never rid myself of. I am not embarrassed to say that while shopping at the supermarket—I wanted to leave you well stocked with supplies—and listening to your vile comments, I was mumbling under my breath, "Oh, God, please take her *soon*."

And yet, the misery was punctuated by moments of tenderness. Such as the day before I was about to leave, when you agreed finally to join me in a café on the boardwalk. After we ordered drinks and some snacks, you curled up on the bench—big black sunglasses still on and the crown of shiny, white hair framing your beautiful face—and fell asleep as if you owned the place. "Cool as an oyster," I thought, taking your picture and instantly sending it off to your granddaughters. "Cool as a cucumber," was their more "up-to-date" reaction . . . I was so proud of you.

For the first time, I had a moment to open my book and rest *with* you—just the two of us in my world. When you later woke up from this most peaceful of naps, we watched the rays of the autumnal sun as it was diving into the water and continued sitting as the darkening evening enveloped us. That is how I want to remember you.

Part IV

A DAUGHTER'S KADDISH

December 22–23

The morning turns out to be far less peaceful. You make me remake the tea three times, and it still isn't good. You call me nonstop with endless little requests, none of which I can perform to your satisfaction. Your newest ideas are to do with "designing" a hospital unit right in your bedroom, together with the equipment required to enable you to pee and be wiped down in bed. I am horrified. Where is the woman who declared repeatedly throughout the years that the moment she wouldn't be able to independently go to the bathroom would be the moment she would end it all with her own hands? Fat chance! We are now in the business of—instead of moving you to a nursing home—building one around you.

By the time I manage to get dressed and out of the house for a break, it is already two o'clock in the afternoon, and I haven't even had a cup of coffee. I arrive to a meeting with a childhood friend looking and feeling like a trauma survivor, distracted, able to talk only about you and your unending demands. The last of which, before I step out the door, is to buy you ricotta cheese. Ricotta cheese. Sure.

I get home a few hours later, ricotta cheese in hand. You are nauseous again, and the cheese is, of course, forgotten. You need to pee. It's yesterday all over again, but worse. You are weaker, and you drag your sticks of legs on the floor, holding onto both my hands supporting you—when I am hit by a déjà vu. This is how my father was half carried to the bathroom over twenty-five years ago—looking equally emaciated—and then his death dragged on for a number of years. And I remember very well how disgusted you were. As I relive the scene with you now, your legs trembling with the effort of carrying your diminished weight, I realize with amazement that you have lost all sense of shame—even with me, your most precious one. You shamelessly expose your body looking like a corpse in an image from concentration camps; you shamelessly pee in front of me and let me pull you back to bed, your lower body naked, lay you down, pull your diaper-like disposable underwear on, roll you over from side to side to be able to get it over the empty skin that was once your butt, which I try not to touch, but accidentally do. I shiver. You let me do that—no, you ask and expect me to do that, you refuse any nurse or caretaker—without hesitation. Whatever we call "dignity," well, you lost it.

This forced physical intimacy takes away from the emotional one. After changing your diapers, touching you in such an uncomfortable way, I no longer have the ability to just sit by you and hold your hand or caress your cheek. I turn around and walk out of the room, trying to collect myself. And I start

*being angry with your stubbornness not to have a proper nurse.
I start hating you for that selfishness which accompanies you
to your last days. And I know we have gone too far. I followed
you too far into this journey. It's time to end my accompanying
you. But how?*

*Night. I am in bed in my tiny childhood room, actually a
walled-in terrace big enough for a single bed and nothing else.
You and my father bought this apartment when I was eight
years old. For forty-three years, traveling about the world,
making Tokyo, New York, and now Paris my home, this one
was, after all, the only stable one. I feel as if I never left. I always
tell my girls, who are growing up on three different continents
and often wondering where they belong, "Home is where Mom
is." So this is where my mom was.*

*As a teenager, sitting here, crying over guys who prom-
ised to, but never called, once even hurling a vase at you in
my agony and frustration, I could not have imagined myself in
the same tiny compartment awaiting your death. As helpless as
I felt earlier today at your announcement that you no longer
can get up from bed to go to the bathroom and will henceforth
pee in bed, I still take comfort in hearing your light snoring
from across the wall. Love, true love, is complex. It is not about
"happiness" or simple, good relationships. It's a multilayered,
multifaceted, endless dimensional labyrinth where love, hate,
compassion, anger, and frustration create a dazzling spectrum
of colors. I love you for your meanness and bitchiness just as
much as for your tenderness and sweet pampering, at times.
I love you because you are difficult and stubborn, bigger than*

life, never dull, original, uneducated, vulgar, brilliant—all at the same time. I love you for the pain you have caused me just as much as for the pleasure. Neither of us ever settled for a rosy lie of a life. We both dug deep into each other, hurting and leaving a mark that won't be erased for as long as one of our twin hearts keeps beating.

You ask me about the cheese you requested yesterday.

"It's in the fridge," I reply.

"What does it look like?"

Intuitively, I know you need to be reassured it really is there, to enjoy it with your eyes if you cannot with your palate.

"Do you want to see it?" I ask.

You nod yes.

I put a tiny morsel, the size of a grain of rice, on a teaspoon and give it to you to lick. You try but cannot swallow even that miniscule portion. "She feels the taste, though," I comfort myself. I show you the container with the whole slice in it.

"Put it in the fridge for tomorrow," you say.

"Okay," I reply.

And I add the cheese to the chestnuts, foie gras, and various fine chocolates, all brought from Paris upon your command, never to be touched.

I am ashamed to say that even though I intended to "starve" while you are dying, to identify with you, the force of my healthy body is stronger than me, and half the chocolate is gone, together with much of the cherry liqueur. I feel guilty enjoying alone these earthly pleasures you loved so much and can no longer share. But I cannot be as pure as I would have liked to be, to mourn you in body and soul. My body, unlike your living corpse, is very much alive.

You are exhausted after your shower. Which may be the last shower you take in this life. You fall into a deep sleep, and I take advantage of the opportunity and go out to the café on the boardwalk where only two months ago, on my most recent visit, you took a nap in an armchair, with your sunglasses on and your regal white hair fluttering in the light breeze. This time I sit there alone. I go to remember you. How cool you were to the very last. But I am ashamed to admit that again, having not eaten all day, hunger conquers, and I have a huge salad and some fried sardines as if no mother of mine were dying of starvation. I betray our unity. I abandon you. I choose to remain on this side of the border. The angry waves crash against the wall lining the boardwalk. The sun sets early. I drink. I eat. I flirt. I live. You are dying. We slowly part.

I get home, and you are sitting up, awake but very quiet. You repeat your intention to pee in bed from now on. I threaten to hospitalize you if you do. We both know I won't. You get upset and disown me from my inheritance for the millionth time. Just before dozing off, you ask me in exasperation, "How much longer will it take?"

"I don't know," I say.

"If one must die, I will," you sigh. "But mine was not a life well lived."

Is it this feeling of incompleteness, of a pointless and unhappy life that was first victim to horrifying circumstances, then followed by foolish waste, that makes it so difficult for you to be at peace? Are you wishing, with these few remaining, laborious breaths, for a last chance to correct the irreversible?

You ask me to turn you on your side but complain that my hand touching you hurts. I am too rough. I adjust your pillows. Once you are comfortable, I cover you with the blanket and you fall back asleep. I am alone. But you are still with me. It's just the two of us, in my childhood home, on our own planet.

December 24

"Can't they give me something to just sleep away the time that is left?" you ask.

I don't answer. It is a question I have asked myself hundreds of times during the last few days. I don't think the doctors would agree to do that. But should I? You don't seem to mind what until just a few weeks ago would have been the unthinkable—that I change your diapers. In fact, the prospect of a long period of convalescence, diapers included, was the very reason you opted to decline the doctors' recommendation to try surgery when the cancer was first diagnosed. You concluded that you would rather die than be reduced to such a humiliating existence. That decision died before you did. What is your true will? The one expressed when you were still a human being, one of us, or this new one, which adjusted with such flexibility to these degrading circumstances?

You are not in pain, but your face is a mask of torture. The bird-like skeletal visage, the empty mouth wide open, still gasping for air. What is a good daughter to do? Try to prolong *this life you still seem to be attached to or do what would be a merciful act of love? I hesitate, waver, but can't reach a conclusion. When you see me getting ready to go out for shopping, you ask me to give you something to help you sleep while I am gone. I hesitate, but give you one of the pills I use for those nights when slumber eludes me. You seem relieved and within minutes I hear a gentle snore. But then, fear strikes me. Isn't your body too weak to handle even one sleeping pill? What is the right dose in your condition?*

When I am back from shopping for the diapers you now regularly need, I am hugely relieved to see you still breathing and then later waking up and ordering me around as usual. But my thoughts scare me. I think I would be able to help you die. I often even think I should. It is my obligation and the last act of love I can perform for you. But even if I am right—and I am not at all certain my resolve would last to that critical moment—I am too scared. I have never committed a serious crime in my life and am not able to now either. The prospect of illegality is too bold for the lawyer in me. Am I a coward? Should I take the risk for you? But I don't. I am hiding behind my doubts, unable to act. I can just watch your suffering and deterioration like a heartless witness.

For heaven's sake, why do you have to be so lucid? So consciously aware of your imminent end? Isn't that the cruelest of tricks nature is playing on you, refusing to numb you, spare you the knowledge, dull the recognition? I want to scream! Freud said one cannot grasp one's own death. But you can definitely suffer the fear thereof crawling all over you like a giant spider. Just a couple days ago while I was looking for a pair of scissors—I needed to cut the diapers off you, it was too difficult to pull them even from under your diminished weight—I asked whether you knew where I could find them.

"In the nightstand, the third drawer on the left," you answered without a moment's hesitation.

I pulled out the drawer and there they were—staring at me from their neatly organized place—just as you indicated. No merciful dementia here to ease the transition. Only icy, razor-sharp lucidity.

From the day we are born, we are fed theatrical romantic nonsense. Even those of us who consider ourselves in possession of a critical mind fall into those sugarcoated traps. Such as the ideal of holding the hand of our loved ones on their death-bed. Giving them comfort with gestures of warmth. You are barely able to whisper some unintelligible words. I follow the Hollywood script and caress your cheek. You raise your bony arm and angrily brush my hand away. I am reminded of my stupidity. I am still playing the scene of attending to the dying according to the script we were brainwashed with. You, on the other hand, are beyond that silly pretense. True to yourself, you are not adhering to your role of the "loving dying mother" in this macabre play. You now probably hate me for being unable—in your mind, unwilling—to help you. You may hate me for remaining alive. I speculate. You may not even care. Hollywood, you are defeated by a dying old witch.

I am left wondering why you couldn't stand my touch. What have I done wrong? Was I too rough and impatient? Or *was it just the sensitivity of your skin that could no longer tolerate any touch?*

"Would you like me to leave you alone?" I ask, like the scolded child I feel.

You nod a very positive yes.

Even as I am ashamed of my childishness, I am still dumb and self-centered enough to be hurt.

Had you known I was writing this, I am fairly sure you would have dismissed it as self-serving and phony. The "mourning" daughter trying to justify her cruelty and inability to properly do the little that needs to be done for you—change diapers and provide ice-cold water. I do it, but grudgingly and with a sense of self-sacrifice. I cannot do more. In your old, sane days, you would have justified me. When my father was ill for years, you fiercely shielded me and did not even allow his sister to notify me of his imminent death. Now you blame me for not being the kind of nurse you never wanted me to become. And I, childish, am arguing my case with you by writing these notes you would have despised me for had you known about them. I am still scared of your judgment.

And I would have still selfishly wished for your love, which you are, in your current state, unable to give. It would be a huge waste of resources, and you have none to spare.

I peek at you from the doorway of your room, fearfully checking every couple of hours whether you are still breathing. Your head is tilted at a strange angle, but I refrain from adjusting its position for fear of disturbing you. I go to the bathroom, located next to your room, the bathroom that from now on is there solely for my use; I don't flush, afraid to disturb your peace. My unmade-up, teary face gazes back at me from one of the dozens of mirrors you installed in the apartment in your narcissist obsession. I see a healthier, thirty-five-years-younger version of you. This is what will be left of you for me to with-hold. Your image imprinted in me. I am not sure I want it.

Four a.m. I am changing your wet diapers in the early dawn, careful to be as gentle as possible when turning you over, trying to divert my eyes from your genitals, which you now expose in front of me without shame, almost as if deliberately. Where is the modesty you exhibited during my childhood, when we bathed together? Then I hear your voice, suddenly regaining its icy clarity and sarcasm:

"Aren't you feeling sorry for yourself?!"

I freeze, speechless. As always, you hit right where it hurts the most. Yes, I do feel sorry for myself. It is not the role of a daughter to do this. I only perform these distasteful tasks to try and keep my promise to you and let you die in your own bed rather than in one of those institutions you abhor. Still, I am ashamed of my pitying my own fate while you are the one who is, in fact, dying. Even half dead, you identify that psycholog-ical soft point and bang, perfect aim. Back in my bed, I hear your peaceful snoring. I start thinking that Monika was right to have cut off all contact with you all those years ago.

You are bitter and angry at the prospect of dying. You did not make peace with it. You are still fighting me, perhaps con-fusing me with death itself. I give you a Xanax I found in my bag in the hopes of calming your anxiety. I offer you food, but *when you refuse it I don't insist. I think it may be better for you to get weaker and weaker. To lower your immunity to death. This time your willpower, that fighting spirit that served you so well during your entire life, may be your worst enemy. There is no way for you to win this battle, only to prolong the agony and pain. I need to find a way to neutralize your strength, to open you to the acceptance of death, to encourage you to go against your nature, to put down the weapons and let death in through the least painful gate. I must protect you from yourself.*

December 27

J ust as I was fed up. Lost patience. Last night I finally fell
asleep at three o'clock in the morning. At four, you banged
with a bottle on the edge of your bed, calling me. You banged
on and on, and I decided that if you had enough energy to bang
for that long, you must be fine. I was too tired to get up and
dreaded encouraging a habit of your waking me up at all hours
of the night just for attention. It is not that different from the
advice we used to get about putting babies to bed and letting
them cry it out if they woke up in the middle of the night. I
ignored that advice with my kids but adopt it now with you.
Same banging followed at six o'clock but for a shorter time, and
I managed to get back to sleep.

The phone rang just before eight. The nurse from the hospice I had tried to hire privately informed me that she could be
here in forty minutes—"would that be convenient?" Of course.
Anything that would spare me changing your diapers this
morning would do.

A young Russian woman arrived and transformed the

physical into spiritual. Under her professional hands, your failing, decaying body was treated to a gentle, purifying wash-down, hair and all, genitals refreshed and rubbed with oint-ment to avoid rashes and bedsores, bedding changed mirac-ulously, and when I reentered the room, I felt you in perfect peace, clean, and elated. I have never seen such a powerful example of matter transcending to higher spheres. In your gratitude, you kissed her hands. When she quoted her modest wage for the work, work that was a million times more valu-able than the legal work I have been remunerated so gener-ously for throughout my professional life—I was embarrassed.

The nurse left, and I could not have loved my own daugh-ters as much as I loved her for the miracle she performed. My mother, radiant and purified. I sat by your bed and looked into your half-shut eyes. Those black diamonds were now covered by a foggy film, your gaze cloudy. And then, thanks to the trans-formation performed by the nurse or perhaps the occurrence of some other mysterious act of grace—as I was sitting by your bed, you took my hands.

Yes, I mocked it as a "Hollywood moment," but since my arrival, I had been craving your motherly love. I knew this was not the time for it. I knew you were the one needing to be cared for. I knew not to expect anything. And I didn't. But I did. And now you took my hands in yours. And then you signaled for me to get closer and you took my face in both your hands and caressed it. And you were my mommy again. You held my face, following the outline of my cheeks, my brow, the soft skin under my chin. You wiped my tears with your index finger, you looked at me and with your other hand pointing at your chest, gestured, I.

And I guessed: "You want to say I love you?"

And you nodded yes.

I was praying for the doctor we were waiting for to walk in the door because the pain was too much to bear, and we held each other and it was your "goodbye" and there was nothing more to say. And all the hell of the last few days, the arguments over taking the medications or not, the demands in the middle of the night—it was all worth it just for this moment of being your little girl for one last time and feeling the river of your love flowing again through the space between us, nourishing me for the remainder of my life.

"I will always love you," I said.

Then, I added: "You can let go. I will be fine."

It was the first time that I lied to you.

You nodded.

The doctor arrived, and I collapsed into his arms. We sat together. There were three of us at your deathbed—the doctor, me, and, of course, you. He, a handsome Arab-Israeli—you often used to tease him, telling him you wished you had been a few years younger—had known you for almost two decades. He cared for your needs as devotedly as a dutiful son, brushing off the hysteria, tantrums, and occasional insults you piled upon him in your heyday. He was, at times, far more compassionate and understanding of your hardship and loneliness than I was. His eyes were tearing as he, too, said his goodbye. He held your hand. You let him hold it. We sat in silence, united for the last time.

"It won't be much longer," he comforted me when we moved into the living room.

With a whisper that was barely audible, but I heard, you summoned me back to your bedroom. You tried pitifully to lift up your head, and your parched lips mouthed, in an enormous effort to be coherent, a plea for the doctor to give you something that would hasten your death. I looked at you lying there exhausted and, almost in shame, apologized.

"He can't do that."

You waved your hand in exasperation and let your head fall back on the pillow in defeat and frustration.

"He can perhaps give you something to cloud your mind. You will sleep and not even know the difference when it turns into death."

You nodded in approval and your facial features relaxed. I wasn't as useless after all.

He gave you a morphine patch. Your eyes followed my hand approvingly as I placed it on your upper back near the right shoulder, making sure it stuck, sending you off with my own loving hands. The sleeping and anti-nausea pills he prescribed were more difficult—you almost choked on them as you tried to swallow, helplessly holding one of your white rags onto your mouth in an effort to keep the pills from being spit out, and I thought we may have waited too long. But knowing their purpose, you used all your strength and resisted throwing up the precious pills. You no longer fought death. You cooperated with it.

"How much longer?" you mouthed.

And I could not lie and offer a comforting answer but was probably right when I said, "Not much longer. I am trying to help you as much as I can without getting in trouble."

And you nodded again in acknowledgement. All those painful dilemmas of the past few days were now settled.

You are on your way. You clearly are now ready to leave me on this shore. We have reached the border between the living and the dead, and only you have the passport. This time I am the one waving from the waiting room. I can accompany you no farther. Here is where we part.

When I had verified that you were sound asleep, that the morphine had not caused any bad side effects, I ventured out of the confines of the apartment for a breath of fresh air. I walked down Rothschild Boulevard, crowded with people strolling around in the mild December weather, a sliver of new moon in the clear evening sky. I was crying, but with acceptance and relief. The end of this agony was in sight, and you and I had said our proper goodbyes. What else could have been said that was not said between your fading crystal eyes and mine? How much more can one person love another? Your finger under my eyes, wiping my tears. We have not been this close and united since I was in your womb.

I want it to end now. At this very moment. But when I am back, your breath is still steady and your heart, ever so strong, keeps beating evenly. You are spread in an awkward position on the bed, and I don't adjust it to avoid inadvertently hurting you. And myself. Nature is indifferent that way. It will keep you alive as long as your heart keeps beating—and it does.

It is a strange scene. Just you and I and this unfinished business of death. No family gathering to say their final goodbyes and no relatives to participate in the vigil. Even my daughters are far away. They are repulsed when I try to communicate to them the gruesome details. For a while, I am upset. Despite my pleas for support, their emails are as short as three words. They consider they are too young to be exposed to the ugly facts of death. I now resent what I perceive to be my "plastic American daughters." Weren't girls their age physically tending to their dying grandparents in other times, other places? Weren't kids supposed to be standing by their dying relatives' bedsides and dealing with the carnal view of death? Did I shield them, keep them away from this experience, supposedly for their own good, to the point that they became the kind of people I can no longer share "real life" with?

Then I remember myself at seventeen. Rushing to your bedside as you woke up from surgery. The doctors had suspected breast cancer and, like most women after such a procedure, you were feeling to see whether or not your breast had been removed following the biopsy. You were exactly my age now and had just lost your best friend to cancer a few months beforehand. Reassured that your breast was still in place, you then struggled to focus a confused gaze on me and asked whether the guy I was infatuated with at the time had called. That was your second immediate concern—my little heartaches and crushes. And, in the same self-centered fashion as my daughters now, I began tiring you with a long and convoluted report about when he called, what he said, how I replied . . . You listened attentively, your hand still feeling your intact breast. No, I was not much better.

I am so lonely here in my childhood home, the one I hate, the one I feel no nostalgia for. My husband asked whether he should fly over, and I declined. I am lonely to the bones but feel that you and I have to complete this journey, just the two of us. No hospitals, no relatives, no neighbors, not even grandchildren. It has always been you and I. And in this bubble of the path to your parting, in this bubble we created our own little happiness, our own little gift of diaper changes, of waiting, a universe consisting of just the two of us, just as you planned. These are our moments, the last ones. And we don't want to share them. I thought it was all in my romantic imagination— that is, until you took my face in your hands tonight.

Mama. It has been a long and painful journey. Please go. I cannot stand it any longer. I will miss you every moment for the rest of my life. Of our lives. But for the sake of our love, please go.

And then the tense muscles guarding your airways from the penetration of death relax and give in. Your eyes allow the dry, invisible tears to be released from their tightly shut pools. You resign. It is no longer a war between us—the one living and the one dying. Now we can love. And I, your daughter, your loved one, am transformed into your priest and angel of death in one—delivering you absolution from this life, sending you off and receiving you with my welcoming arms wide open across the bridge of fire. With your eyes now sunk deeper into their sockets, you hold onto my hand and I carefully help you cross. I hope the morphine is giving you a good trip, the first and last in your otherwise drug-free life. You are immobile other than the heavy breathing. Slowly, we now have time, walk as slowly as you need, blindly and in what I am hoping is a surreal, painless, and peaceful journey to the other side. You are not alone as you had feared. I realize we are never alone on our deathbed. The angel of death, in whatever form, wearing whatever mask—even that of your loving daughter—is lurking at your head, guarding and counting your last breaths.

Bath and Tea (Pause)

It started in my early childhood during the frozen Transylvanian winters, with that wooden basin hidden under the bed and filled with water that was heated in pots over the kitchen stove. I looked forward to those naked soaks, splashing water around, laughing and ignoring your hopeless scolds about the floor getting all wet. I knew I was too cute—and you were too lenient—to be punished. It continued over the years, by now in a proper bathtub, my childish nakedness sharing the warmth with your ripe fullness. Your washing my hair, my attempts to wash your thick, still mostly black mane, with short, stubby fingers. Your blowing big, fat soap bubbles in front of my astonished eyes while I get frustrated in my failing attempts to produce any; forming a lathery circle between my thumb and index finger, the foam explodes before having a chance to materialize into a ball. Those sensations are replicated thirty years later with each of my daughters—to vanish into memory as well. Now I end each day with a deep, warm bath. The ritual around it—filling up the tub while I take off my clothes, raise my hair and tie it in a chignon, clean my nostrils, brush my teeth. All the while, the water flowing in a pleasant, steady stream. I test the temperature, adjusting if it is too hot. Then I submerge myself in the inviting warmth, letting it envelop me, wash away the poison of the day. I lower myself until my shoulders are fully covered, careful not to wet my hair. My thighs, my belly, my breasts all welcome the lightness, being buoyed, floating. My senses are overwhelmed with the sensuality that caresses me, the tiny waves play against my skin. Things cannot be that bad. No matter how difficult it may seem, the luxury of taking a bath, of having a bath, hot water, the ability to cleanse and warm oneself, is not to be taken for granted.

I am not marching in the snow in desperate search of a temporary safe haven, nor am I cold or hungry. I am not escaping bloodthirsty dogs in the woods. I am not being lured into fake showers. We walk past the homeless as if they belonged to a different planet. I, however, know that any slip off this tightrope balancing act can land me among them. I don't even have to slip. Someone may just randomly, indifferently, cut the rope from under me or offer a gentle push into the abyss. Any moment still on it is a miracle to be cherished. I am one of the few fortunate to be able to soak in a warm bath, to luxuriously soap my body, to let the waters penetrate every cell, abandon myself to earthly pleasure. We are living the exception, not the rule.

I let my head rest on the border of the tub, I let my skin be wet, I let my soul relinquish all the dirt that has accumulated within—I purify myself. Then I soap, playing an intimate game with my body, the armpits, the breasts, my vagina, in between the buttocks—and take a last dive before pulling the plug to let the water drain. All red and steaming, I step out onto the rug and dry myself with a big white towel. I look at my flushed face in the mirror just over the sink, my body a bit too full and starting to soften, glistening in its own light. I let my hair fall down on my shoulders and I am grateful for the life I have. Not perfect, but far from bad.

Apparently, caffeine—and its effect on babies—was not a concern in Romania of the 1960s. My bottles were filled with sweet, lemony tea that you believed soothed my tummy. Not quite gourmet, but nevertheless the beginning of a lifelong love affair.

The process has evolved, and now I have dozens of teas to choose from. Delicate white. Chinese green infused with fresh mint. A lovely Darjeeling to be savored pure. Dark black or Earl Grey to be enjoyed with a creamy coat of milk. And, of course, Japanese green tea—divided into various grades, culminating in Gyokuro, so delicate that one can eat the leaves after brewing. Having all those choices fills me with sumptuous anticipation as I walk into the kitchen in the morning. While the water is boiling in the kettle, I search and contemplate my inner mood. Clear and monastic calls for a pure green. A bit playful allows for adventures with Chinese oolong or a Pu-ehr. Indulgent and spoilt calls for a soothing Scottish breakfast. Anxiety and disquiet can be dealt with a perfumed Indian chai. I pick out the proper pot. Each is

chosen carefully to be in harmony with the tea it is to gestate, each infused with the unique aroma that has penetrated
its pores over years of use. I caress each vessel, pour boiling
water to heat it up, and then discard. I measure the leaves and
let them sweat in the steamy pot.

Most teas require a temperature below boiling point, so I
have time to brush my teeth while the water is cooling down to
the right level. I carefully pour the water into a cup, then into
the pot. One should be careful not to shock the leaves with a
violent, wet encounter. I let it steep just the right amount of
time—no longer than sixty seconds for green, four minutes
for black, and up to fifteen minutes for certain Chinese teas—
the rolled leaves take a while to stretch after the long confinement in the tin. Choosing the right cup is another delightful
decision to make. Coarse Japanese ceramic, sensual, so rough
and uneven in the hand that it almost scratches my skin as I
passionately run my finger along its surface; or smooth and
rather cold, flowery English porcelain.

Just at the right moment, not too soon, when my palate
is eager enough, yearning, I take the first sip. The thirst,
nightmares, fatigue are washed away as the refreshing brew
penetrates my inner parts. I can feel it flowing down into my
digestive system, comforting my battle-scarred heart, fueling my lungs to keep pumping air, watering my intestines,
warming me from the inside, healing my soul. Life's basic
pleasures—warmth and nourishment culminate in that first
cup of tea of the day.

You were the fountain of pleasure to the child I was.

Nowadays, my teas are light-years away from the syrupy, lemon-infused liquid of my childhood, but they stem directly from rituals you introduced me to, carrying cup after cup to my room, each cup leading to a chat, each chat another stitch in the fabric of our closeness. And so it ended. With those last sweetened cups I carried to your bedside—offering tiny sips of comfort to your failing body.

Little Lego pieces of pleasure—accompanying us from babyhood to our final, feeble days. And far more than our haughty pursuits and heroic achievements, a warm bath and a cup of tea are all we crave and can rely on when all else fades.

December 28

For four years I have been expecting your death. I knew it would hurt. I could not have imagined how much. This morning I was still thinking it would never end, I would be changing diapers for weeks to come, you would be waking me in the middle of the night for another this or that which would never satisfy you. And then, after four long years of waiting, it is so sudden. I walk in from what is now my usual "break" on the boardwalk. I sat in the same café that has become a sort of memorial site, a memorial to your happier days, napping in the sun. I remember how you regretted not going there more often. Too late to remedy that. Too late to remedy anything now.

I walk in and notice you in the very same position as when I left you in the morning. Your breath is even, your chest rising and falling gently. But your eyes are sunken as if withdrawn into their sockets. When you stir briefly and your hand goes automatically to your diapers, I am so grateful to see you moving that I happily change them for you. As I turn you on your side to pull them off, I notice the bedsores, ugly red spots on your back and buttocks. I gently wipe the spots. Hard to believe that only ten days ago I averted my eyes, disgusted by the sight of the skin drooping from your skinny behind. Now I spread some cream before expertly pulling on a fresh pair of disposable panties, rolling you from side to side to better adjust them. I do it willingly, as a last gesture of love. But I am rolling almost a cadaver, your body as disconnected as a pile of rags.

I tell you that Mia, your granddaughter, is on her way, and you nod. Yes, that "plastic American" daughter surprised me by coming to witness the very details she was so reluctant to hear about over the phone. The minute I gave her "permission" to join me, she did not hesitate, packed, and got on the first flight. As usual, I was too harsh and hasty with my judgment. I ask you to wait for Mia and you nod again. I ask you whether you understand me and you nod. I am relieved. I tiptoe into your room every half hour or so to check on your breathing. Was it I who just this morning wished to hasten your death? Almost a reality, I now can't stand the prospect.

I notice your arms moving; the hands seem enormous protruding from the skinny sticks of your arms. I touch your hand and, startled, you open your eyes a crack, clearly coming back from far away. Your eyes are now covered with a thicker gray film. I talk to you, and you no longer react. I ask whether you would like a sip of water and you do nod, but when I try to let you hold the cup, remembering how you always insisted on it, you no longer grip the handle. I try pouring some water into your mouth with a spoon, but you are not swallowing and I am afraid of choking you. In desperation, I wet a piece of cotton, *squeeze it into your mouth—no movement. You don't even lick your lips as the drops spill out. Your tongue seems black in your mouth, but I am afraid to look. You fall back asleep and your breath is still even. I notice you are very warm, burning with high fever. I document it all.*

I had always hoped to wake up and find you had died in your sleep. "Death by a kiss" it is called in Hebrew. Now I cannot leave you. I am sitting on the floor by your bed, facing the big Marilyn Monroe poster, the kitschy, cheap landscape paintings hanging around it, the framed photos of Monika, me, my girls, and of course photos of you posing proudly in one shiny, bright-colored outfit or another—the blue dress, the tight red sweater with black boots. And now in your white bed, white linen, white hair. This is the death you orchestrated for yourself. And I played it under your baton to the last note, performed your instructions to the letter. Perfection. The suffering was probably not in the score. The ugliness of it all was not predicted either. The diapers, for example, were certainly not in the original script, though you did adapt to them remarkably well once introduced. Overall, you were the master of your destiny to your last minute. Down to your fingernails, still manicured and polished with a pearly veneer.

Last night I went through some photos and the very few notes you did not throw away in your cleanliness mania. One, from my father, apologetic, promises:

"It will never happen again, please enjoy the gift"—probably a piece of jewelry you received as "compensation" after one of his bouts of violence.

Letters from me. As a young mother in Tokyo or New York—I wrote to you as if I were a five-year-old adoring her idol mom. Wherever I was, I always sent you photos with handwritten explanations on the back—who was in the picture and where it was taken. These last few days did not come out of nowhere. I loved you as few do, well beyond the age we find endless fault in our parents. The madness and banging of phones must have come much later.

We are back at square one. I count each inhalation. I am startled every time you stir. Will there be an end to this longest of nights?

Sleeping on the floor by your bed, I wake up a couple of hours later and am hesitant to check whether or not you are still breathing. Ignorance may give me a few more hours of rest. I check anyway, and the shallow breaths are continuing uninterrupted. Was it you—the one summoning me, banging a bottle against the side of your bed just a few nights ago? Those arms—now moving about involuntarily, gripping the air—are not able to lift a feather, let alone a bottle. I am so lonely. You are no longer with me. The shallow breaths are barely audible.

I look around me at this universe we locked ourselves in. Total isolation. Just the two of us. Unnoticed, I built a sort of shelter where I stashed enough cold drinks and diapers for you; vodka, food, and books for me, to outlast a siege. And this messy makeshift bed on the floor next to yours to guard you. A stranger knocking on the door and stepping in would have thought I had lost my mind. And I probably had. But no one knocked. No one stepped in to chase away the spell. We were undisturbed in this parallel world of ours—created and maintained by me to be a no-man's-land—in between life and death. A land that is a hanging bridge. And on this bridge, just as Jacob struggled all night long with the angel of God, you and I struggled with his other messenger. We were silently united in embrace—you, me, and death. Jacob won the battle and was rewarded with a new name—Israel. You tried to hold on to your original maiden name—Izrael. But slyly I betrayed you and, unbeknown to you, sided with death. Defeated, we lie here all three, motionless, helpless, in anticipation as the bridge sways quietly to the rhythm of your peaceful last breaths.

I wait. As a new day dawns, the support systems come in. Mia is in midair, only a couple of hours away. My cousin cancels all her plans and is on her way. We will no longer have the intimacy we shared. I regret losing it. But I know it is time to part. You will continue on to the place where not even shallow breaths are required, and I will rejoin the living. And these last weeks will be stored in the drawers of our forever united memories.

December 30

did my research. I knew what to expect. I found a Canadian virtual hospice website describing the final stages in detail, and that information provided me with some comfort. I could recognize the signs—the high fever, the swelling of the ankles—and felt less at a loss as to what to expect. So when the loud, automatic, machine-like breaths arrived early Friday morning, I knew it was the stem brain taking over, the cognitive part shutting down. Your chest went up and down as if pumped by a mechanical device, fast and deafening. I had to move to the other room to get on the phone to make funeral arrangements. It was clear those would be called for within the hours to come. Minutes later, when I went back to check on you, the room was quiet. You were silent and your breast no longer rose or fell.

I waited a few moments and then called for the ambulance and medics. Within minutes the sirens were screaming up and down the street and the apartment was filled with strangers, rushing, violently stepping on your perfectly vacuumed carpets, attacking your death bed with a gush of activity, insisting *against my pleas to try to revive you, piercing our carefully constructed peace. You no longer cared, I hoped. Nor did you notice—atheist that you were—the two devout, long-bearded Orthodox neighbors swaying back and forth in prayer, accompanying your soul as the faint pulse in your veins faded away.*

Then, all mandatory questions being answered (for a moment I was afraid the police officer would accuse me of causing your death—I had no witnesses to testify to my innocence), forms filled, the whole lot vanished just as abruptly as they had appeared. Only their footprints, which would have driven you to distraction, were left as reminders of death's very recent visit, and the air, stirred by the noise and action, soon settled to an empty hush. An hour or so later, a crude lone employee of the funeral services company rang the doorbell, loaded you onto a stretcher, and whisked you away to be refrigerated over the weekend. And you were no more.

Session 24

Darkness

January 4, 2014

My suitcase is packed. It is my last night at your apartment. You have been dead for almost a week, and I still talk to you. We actually had a pause during the past few days. Mia's arrival, which you may or may not have been aware of, the nurse cleaning your body one last time, the two nights I spent sleeping on the floor in your room, counting your breaths. I was hoping you might still wake up to acknowledge Mia—who, with the same complexion and similar features was the closest stand-in for Monika, your absent daughter. Startled by the fast, heavy, automatic breaths, realizing that we were near the end and making a phone call to see that arrangements were made—it was Friday and most services in Israel are shut down by noon; returning to your room to find you no longer breathing. The ambulance, the arguments with the overzealous medical staff wanting to resuscitate you, someone pulling the blanket to cover your face, your body being taken away. It all happened in a cloud of foggy, intense activity.

I could no longer talk to you. There were too many people surrounding us. And then Mia and I spent the weekend trying to clear our heads from the illness that seemed to be stuck to us like a second layer of clothing. We were mostly in the fresh air on the boardwalk, away from the smell of decay and death. We didn't sit shiva, the seven-day, at-home mourning period that Jewish custom requires. With whom? And what for? I didn't need the hollow condolences and empty sympathy of acquaintances or near strangers. Mourning is a universe of its own; only those residing in it feel the pain. And I was mourning you while walking down the street, sitting in a café, in the privacy of the bathroom, and in the full view of all of Tel Aviv. I did not need to sit on the floor. I could have danced and still been mourning you.

We sometimes overdid it, and on New Year's Eve, I ended up falling drunkenly into a ditch and almost breaking my back. I made it to your funeral nauseous and numb to the bones. I identified your body; knowing how vain you were when alive, I figured you'd rather not be seen by anyone other than me in your grotesque death mask—your waxy, yellowish skin and open, toothless mouth.

"I remember her well," the undertaker volunteered as he was untying the white cloth that covered your hard-to-recognize face. "She used to come regularly to clean up and attend to her husband's grave. I haven't seen her around much lately, though . . ."

He was an expert witness to your changing role from visitor of the cemetery to resident.

Before your actual death, whenever I used to imagine your funeral, I would be overcome by tears. Even as a theoretical notion, it was too painful to contemplate. I could not see how I'd possibly be able to contain such sorrow without jumping into the grave with you, covering myself with the earth that was to be swallowing you. In reality, I walked to the gravesite calm and composed, drained of all emotion. My hand in Mia's, holding onto her. Her delicate frame supporting my weight. An Orthodox neighbor said the Kaddish. I remembered with gratitude the unexpected comfort his prayer by your bedside—the ancient ritual that was packaging your death with all those preceding it, sending you peacefully into the welcoming embrace of the universe—had brought Mia and me. And then your body, suddenly so small, was swallowed by the open hole in the ground.

That body was not you. That body was not my beautiful, chubby mother. That body was a stranger, an impersonator. I felt no relationship to it. They put a shovel in my hands and told me to scoop some earth into the open grave, and I felt as ridiculous as if I were playing in a sandbox. One of our laugh-death-in-the-face comments was forming in my head and I needed all my self-restraint to keep it from escaping my lips; no one but you would have been amused. More consoling words from the few old friends who are nowadays attending each other's funerals, waiting for their own lottery number to be called. A distant cousin, whose parents are buried near your resting place, offered an almost lyrical resignation, joking about all of you lying in such proximity that enables you to resume your weekly Remy card games. I found more consolation in his black humor than in all the expressions of condolences. And the small gathering parted.

I accepted your neighbor's offer to organize a group of religious scholars to say Kaddish at your (hereafter, former) home. The suggestion was so touching in its gentle, unimposing manner that I had no heart to refuse. I figured it couldn't hurt. You used to enjoy the religious chanting that penetrated your sinner's cave from neighboring synagogues, reminding you of the times you still had a real home, one with a mother and father in it. As it turned out, a whole busload of bearded, black-clad men, enthusiastic to gain some points with the Almighty, descended upon your apartment and, all facing east toward Jerusalem, ushered your soul in its ascent to heaven. Though an invisible hand had swiftly covered the statue that was on the terrace—just between those holy men and their God—with some black cloth, it still seemed as if that nude idol were the immediate object of their worship. If you had, indeed, encountered God, you two must have had a good laugh.

The last few days, you left me. Or I left you. There were endless administrative chores to attend to, lawyers to meet, keys to hand over, and Mia kept me company. You stayed away. My heart was as empty as your bed. Only now, on my last night in your apartment, my home, you slowly tiptoe back. Or do you? Is it you I am still talking to? Do you still feel me? The memory of your bony hand caressing my face, your fading eyes looking into mine, is gaining ground over the death mask I identified at the cemetery.

I take little with me. Some photos, old records, loving letters I wrote you. The rest remains untouched. Those artificial flowers I fantasized about throwing out as soon as you were dead are exactly where they were, not one petal missing. The cheap, ugly pictures are still hanging on the walls, and the carpets are layered one on top of the other, hiding every inch of floor. Your bed is covered with the same white satin bedcover, with the three white roses Mia picked from all those plastic flowers being the only addition. You would have been pleased seeing those roses placed on your bed. I mocked you when you asked me to keep the apartment "as is" for a while after your death. I thought I would spare no time in getting rid of all that dust-accumulating kitsch. And now it is a shrine to your memory. Oh, yes—you would have been pleased. Victorious to the end and even beyond.

It is our last night here. At least for a while. And then this apartment that has been my only stable home will be closed and sold. And you? Where will you be? I suspect that I will carry you with me on the plane back to Paris as an invisible passenger. We will, most likely, continue our never-ending conversation. We will just no longer need a phone.

You once promised to stay with me for as long as I needed you. I am now going to find out whether you are to keep that promise.

Session 25

Phantom

January 5, 2014

T el Aviv airport was our point of departure. Since that day, twenty-five years ago—when I boarded a plane, two half-empty suitcases in hand—we have been saying our perpetual, emotional goodbyes at this airport. Your figure shrinking, your back no longer as erect, your hair acquiring its white brilliance no longer mixed with black. As you got older and frailer, each time we wondered if and when we would see each other again. And we always did. Time after time you conquered God, fighting Him back with your venom and chasing Him away. Each time there was another time.

No wonder this too seems like another false alarm. But now I only have the memory of you standing in white pants, black top, and shining white hair, waving and crying as I walk away toward the security checkpoint; those dozens of times all mix together into one replay of the same departure—your tears, our frantic waves until we could no longer see each other, and my secret sigh of relief when I no longer had to bear witness to your pain. Year after year. You fought your weakness, insisting on escorting me even when I had to put you in a taxi to take you home as soon as we arrived at the airport. After that, your lonely figure waved to me as I drove away in my rental car down the path leading from your apartment to the main road—away from you, from the burden you had become. And each time—in a replay of walking away from my father's hospital bed—"Is this the last I see of you?"

How many goodbyes can two hearts bear?

Earlier this morning I locked the apartment, and you no longer stood on the street to wave. I drove away saying no goodbyes. I could still see you at the airport, at the same exact spot you had always stood, but you waved only in my imagination. I went through security and didn't turn back.

The cemetery, the funeral—all those were an abstract performance, a macabre spectacle I participated in, going through the motions. This airport was our real home. It was here that we accumulated our memories, our comings and goings; with first husband, second child, divorced, alone, richer, with second husband, older, going through the cycles of life. The points where we met were the only constant.

It really is over. There will be no miraculous recovery, no rising from the dead. Next time I come you will no longer be there to greet me with your eternal stuffed cabbage and Hungarian desserts that I ended up schlepping back with me in plastic containers from continent to continent. I will be greeted only by the furniture, the carpets, the pictures on the wall, silent figurines living behind the glass cabinet in the salon, and your absence.

I won't lie. It is a tremendous relief. Not to have to make that obligatory daily phone call or risk your wrath. Not to worry constantly whether I would be summoned for an emergency visit because of a drop in the hemoglobin levels. I can plan a vacation without worrying about having to cancel it due to a sudden hospitalization. That constant sword hanging over my head has finally dropped, and I can rest my fears. But I cannot rest my pain.

And I cannot erase the guilt and longing as I still see you standing at the airport, on the street corner, waving, always alone as I leave you behind.

This is the first time I am not leaving you. You left me. I am going home, to my current, provisional home—wherever it now happens to be—back to my normal life. Back to a daughter I will be waving goodbye to in a few years as she slowly detaches from me. Back to the routine. The keys to my childhood home are still in my bag, but not for long. It will soon be put up for sale, the contents given away or scattered randomly. It should not matter much, as I haven't lived in that apartment for twenty-five years, and the memories I have of it are far from sweet. "Good riddance," I should say and probably will. Yet I may be surprised, just as I was surprised at my inability to fulfill my dream of throwing away your garden of artificial flowers. Our blood runs thick. Your presence is still here, forbidding me to disobey you, even beyond the grave.

Your hold over me will gradually wane. I should hope so, for my sanity's sake. But, for the moment, I am sitting on a crowded plane amid crying babies and foul smells of airline food, and I am talking to you, carrying you as overweight luggage inside.

Session 26

Dreams

I wake up every morning and have a few moments of reprieve and blissful ignorance until the knowledge of your death resurfaces and grips my throat in violent awareness. Each and every morning you die again. And again.

In my dreams, you are still alive. Correction. I *do* know that you have died, but you are still with me. You show up every night—younger, healthier, gentler than in your final years—and you keep me company.

Elise was about two years old, naked, chubby, dancing on her tiptoes. Mia was there too, in a good mood, about twelve years old, round glasses and braces adorning her childish face. In fact, it felt like the time of our grand European tour when all four of us spent a couple weeks traveling around Budapest, Vienna, and Prague together. In my dream, we were relaxed and having a pleasant time. It was then that I wondered whether I should talk to you about it or perhaps it would be bad timing—I didn't want to spoil your high spirits, but on the other hand, I thought it might cheer you up to know. I asked you whether you would like to talk about it, but you didn't quite understand my question, so I went ahead and told you that you were going to die peacefully, with no pain, sleeping in your own bed. I saw the image in front of my eyes—your bed as Mia last made it, the three white roses on the white background of your blanket—and I tried to convey it to you. I told you I was certain of it because just three weeks ago I had been there, by your deathbed. I was somehow in both time zones at once—*with* you in that moment and *past* your death. You didn't seem to quite grasp what I was saying and replied with a nonchalant, "Good."

But I was glad I got to tell you.

Another night, we were on a picnic and you looked happy. We talked and talked, your tone very kind to me, and at a certain point I even lay down on you, curled up with my head on your outstretched legs.

I said, "So the fact that you are now dead only means that you will always be with me—always—and we can chat like this all the time?"

You said, "Yes."

"And," I continued, "does that mean I am getting older because I am still alive while you stay the same?"

You smiled softly and nodded.

I see you on your white deathbed. You are still and composed as a picture. I know you took your own life—as you had always planned—by swallowing a bottle of sleeping pills. You look peaceful lying there and I am grateful for your consideration, for sparing me the horror of accompanying you through your death throes, for this last gesture of love. I wake up.

There is not one night you don't join me. The girls are much younger—and so are you. I am the only one getting older, and the years are heavy on my shoulders. I know someday you will part from my dreams as well. I hope it won't happen for a while yet—not before you judge me old enough to be left alone.

Isn't it when one's mom dies that we start getting older? The biochemical agents that have thus far inhabited your body hopped over and drifted slowly along the bloodstream into my veins, burrowed themselves into my cells, and promptly started their destructive labor to wrinkle my skin, dry out my hair and drain it of its color, bloat my stomach, and put extra weight around my knees. It's my turn to become you.

Session 27
As Time Goes By. . .
Paris, Spring 2014

Elise is on stage. Wearing a short dress, her body is in the crossing between childhood chubbiness and womanly curves. Her long, dark, wavy hair crowns a still somewhat roundish and radiant face. This miracle child of mine with the perfect pitch. You were the one to first notice her exceptional talent when the four of us were driving on badly paved country roads between Vienna and Prague. I was distracted by the potholes when you, after an unusually long silence, said, "Listen to Elise. She has a crystal-clear voice and an amazing range. She sings beautifully."

I dismissed it with a shrug—who pays attention to a two-year-old inventing songs in the back seat of a car, pretending to be an opera singer?

"Don't neglect it!" you kept insisting.

Your keen observation, coming from a woman who had not had one single music lesson in her life, has been confirmed by many singing teachers over the years. How could you have been so maddeningly right about *everything*?

You hummed that tune, the theme melody from *Casablanca*, as you held your granddaughters under your arms on that horror of Seder nights. As if such transformation were a normal continuation of your madhouse performance of just minutes earlier, you poured your love into their young, receptive hearts. Elise asked to sing that same song at her end-of-year concert. Up on stage, she fights her tears as I do mine back in the audience, but her voice is bright and confident. "As time goes by . . ." Here's looking at *you*, Mom!

A few days earlier, entering what seemed to be the fiftieth shop, looking for a dress for the performance, I sank into an armchair strategically placed near the dressing rooms. Elise went in and out of the booth, parading one outfit after the other. Exhausted, I nodded briefly a short yes or no indicating my approval or displeasure, waving as if an impatient baton. I glanced at myself in the mirror—middle-aged, just slightly on the heavy side, long, unruly hair, clearly opinionated—and saw you. I saw you sitting, year after year, as I had been posing in front of you, modeling clothes, shoes, waiting for that quick nod, your swift, determined judgment. Was it me or was it you in that armchair? Our respective silhouettes blend into one another, our impatient motions indistinguishable. We nod in unison, head tilted a bit to the right or to the left. Our combined weight drops deeper into the seat, our eyes measure, our hand signals, yes and no and no and yes and yes and yes . . .

I wanted to write of our separation. I ended up writing of us becoming one. And how I came to be at peace with it.

Part of me died with you. Part of you lives on within me. The cell exchange that occurred in the womb means that you *are* physically residing in me. The cells that traveled from my bloodstream died in your veins. And the fusion did not stop at the gates of death—I just became a little *more* you. Complexity does not negate; on the contrary, it rather empowers—love.

I wanted to tell your story. To give you a voice. I ended up telling *our* story—the two inseparably intertwined. Have I done you justice? Have I faithfully represented you? I will never know. You are no longer here to either scold or be proud of me. Going forward, it is only *my* story, which occasionally feels almost meaningless to conceive without you cheering from the sidelines. Without you it feels that all my words will be hollow, an echo of my cry for you: "Mama."

Would I ever be able to talk of you in the third person?

Part V

WITNESS

The World of Yesterday

Rural Transylvania, early 1930s

A little girl, you were entrusted to a local peasant, perched on the back of his horse-drawn cart to take you to your grandparents' farm. An airplane flying by was a rare and magical sight; a car drew hordes of kids running in its wake. The earth, saturated with the gallons of blood it had absorbed during the previous Great War, lay content, yielding abundant harvests—ignorant of the future not-so-great war, which would further fertilize its bottomless hunger with ashes. In the eastern provinces of the former Austro-Hungarian Empire, yellowing blades of wheat continued their lazy dance to the rhythm of a soundless czardas, and men greeted their ladies with a gallant *kezi csokolom*, "I kiss your hand," followed by a deep bow and a slight touch of lips to the naked skin. Once safely deposited in front of the isolated wooden farmhouse crowned with a thatched roof, the adjacent, vast orchards became your kingdom, the cows and horses your subjects, for the remainder of the summer months. Until the autumn winds called to make the trip back to town and to the cramped two rooms shared with four siblings, all ranking higher than you in age or gender.

The taste of those long-ago apples must have lingered in your mouth half a century later on an apple-picking trip in upstate New York; frolicking hand-in-hand with your own five-year-old granddaughter, your legs forgetting the thick layers of flesh draping them, you bit into every apple and ended up with a tummy ache. As if the recent pages had been erased from the history books, only to allow you one more dreamlike afternoon.

"I hated my grandmother," you confessed, whispering as if she could still hear you. "She was dark, skinny, and mean. She would lock me up at night in the barn as punishment. I was so scared."

An offended child still resided in your wrinkled eyes.

"She was jealous because my grandfather loved me more!" You continued hissing and stole a sideways look in case your nemesis came back from the dead.

Winters meant sleigh rides, skating, housekeeping chores, and needlework. From time to time, your mother would take a moment to praise the tiny stitches on an embroidered napkin, caressing your cheek with the tip of her finger and calling you softly by your Hebrew name, Malka'leh. Soon, the majority of the land, the vineyards and plum distilleries had been sold or signed away, the money squandered by your father. The spoiled offspring of an unorthodox love union between a daughter of the Hungarian aristocracy and a Jewish man, he had been raised by his mother to live the idle life of the social milieu she had grown up in. Off he went to pursue some vague artistic aspirations in Paris, leaving his own young family behind. Alas, the pleas from his wife to join him in the city of lights were met with a firm refusal. She wouldn't hear of uprooting her life, abandoning her own aging parents and the only place she'd ever called home to follow her husband's follies. That was where she drew the line. He returned—with nothing but some revolutionary ideas and Bohemian manners to show for his labors. You all remained together in that bucolic yet unsuspecting little Transylvanian town.

Strolling through the Musée d'Orsay on an idle Sunday afternoon, I happened upon an exhibition dedicated to Hungarian artists of the early twentieth century who were part of the Fauvist movement. I learned that groups of Transylvanian musicians and painters—influenced by their experiences abroad, mainly in Paris—formed a new movement within the European avant-garde and, as the brochure explained, "created their own distinctive idiom, a modernity imbued with the traditions of Hungary." This resonated with your account, and I canvassed the names on the little plaques describing the pieces in an attempt to discover a trace of the blue-eyed grandfather I knew only from your romanticized depictions of him. In vain.

The war drew closer. In 1940, Northern Transylvania, often changing hands but under Romanian rule since 1919, reverted to Hungary. Jewish men were soon condemned to join the forced-labor battalions and sent off to the east. The nightly air was thick with voices of the young recruits serenading their sweethearts under the windows, promising eternal love and a bright future upon their return. Few would. Disregarding the danger of exhibiting the portrait of a Jewish girl, the owner of the local photography shop could not resist placing your enlarged image at the window display. Your beauty—with the long black curls and radiant eyes—was legendary. So was your girlish vanity. Despite your sisters' pleas, you snubbed your admirers by offhandedly refusing to follow custom and light candles to be placed on the window-sill. Peter, one of the lot, would later reminisce how he had endured the mines, hunger, slave labor, and torture with only the memory of your face to sustain and guide his broken body back home. His devotion remained unrequited.

"Neither of you looks like me," you would subsequently declare—referring to Monika and me—in triumphant disappointment.

All Jews were ordered to leave home within three days and crammed into a former brick factory. You watched your mother circling the barbed-wire fence in search of an escape. She was still unaware of the coming horrors that were only a couple weeks ahead; merely the brutality of the guards bode trouble and gave rise to an obscure unease. But the net had been cast and the strings pulled firmly around the hopelessly squirming community.

Packed into cattle cars, you were transported by train to an unheard-of destination. The day before arrival, Willy, your nine-year-old brother, begged for, and your mother surren-dered, an additional slice of bread.

"But it's supposed to be for tomorrow," you complained, betraying your own hunger.

She hushed you with a sigh. For him, there would be no tomorrow.

That brief exchange between you and your mother was one of the rare accounts you confided in my childish ears, perhaps in search for a belated pardon or acquittal. "I didn't know. I was only thinking of *his* well-being . . ."

There is no guilt more persistent than that of the victim.

The train stopped. Frantic shoving and pulling. Dogs barking. You could hear your father, grouped with the men, shout above the noise and confusion, "Are you all together?"

You no longer were.

You didn't talk about that year. But the terrors crept up at night, haunting your nightmares. As a child, I was habitually startled from my own dreams by a sudden scream, then silently listened as you gasped for air on the other side of the thin Sheetrock wall. I never gave an inkling of the fact that I heard. You tried to protect me from those images as if they were a contagious disease. As if that war had left a shameful virus in your blood, forever contaminated. And you were right. And wrong. I was already doomed. Born infected with the virus multiplying rapidly in my veins.

The war was over and your parents were ashes.

You were nineteen. Hastily married off, you gave birth

to a baby girl your husband named Monika, after the child he had lost to the gas chambers. Scarred, unable to be either wife or mother, you played with your daughter as if she were a doll, dressing her in lace-embroidered clothes, curling her hair and tying it in bows. An ugly divorce was followed by yet another unhappy marriage.

You were thirty-five. Drained from a life that contained more tragedies and disillusions than one young woman could sustain on her own. You climbed up to the attic, the content of a bottle of pills melting in your stomach. Noticed by the maid, you were saved—just to prolong your hollow existence.

And that's when I joined you.

You feared for me, this late child of yours, in a primal way. In the neurotic and hysterical way of someone who had seen babies starved, suffocated, burnt, you were—more than loving—just battling to keep this one alive. When I failed to thrive on the nourishment your weakened body was able to produce, there were hurried trips to a Romanian peasant woman who sold you her plentiful milk, with Monika and my father taking turns rushing home so that the precious substance did not spoil in the heat of the July sun. My father was sent looking for rare oranges you could not afford—this was, after all, Eastern Europe in the early 1960s—in an effort to fortify me with vitamin C. When, at three months old, I still failed to put on weight, you shut the door and windows so no one could witness your desperate "crime" and chewed chicken liver to a mush, stuffing tiny portions into my tooth-less mouth, washing it down with lots of sugary tea. It worked.

And you no longer were alone.

Unlike with Monika, you transformed into a doting mother with me. I was a red-faced sponge, soaking up and reradiating your sometimes suffocating but always comfort-ing love. With that earlier lesson of your brother begging for that last slice of bread forever etched in your cells, everything I asked for—chocolate, a doll, a new dress—materialized before I had finished my sentence. Alone among my friends' parents, you never negotiated a "later" or "tomorrow." The future was an uncertain, unreliable, questionable concept, no more than a chance to win the lottery, but with far slimmer odds. With the war, a whole tense was eliminated from our grammar, leaving us with a "past" we tried to chase away as if it had never been and a "present" we didn't trust to last.

You placed all your ambitions on my tender shoulders. I became your *raison d'*être, an innocent collaborator in pro-viding a meaning to your otherwise wasted life. You woke up at dawn to meticulously iron my only school uniform, pulled up my socks and dressed me while I was lying still half asleep in bed, escorted me all the way to school carrying my bag, heavy with books. You waited for me at noon to fly imaginary airplanes loaded with schnitzel and mashed potatoes into my unwilling mouth. You sat in the living room by my side every afternoon, your hands always industriously occupied, knitting or crocheting, while I practiced the piano. You made me perform at each of your card game soirees while the guests dutifully applauded as if they were music connoisseurs and I the next Martha Argerich. You listened while, as part of my homework, I recited poems by heart in a language you were deaf to; by then we had moved to Israel, a land where you were practically illiterate. You slept with me every night until I finally rebelled, without ever suspecting that I had been a convenient excuse to avoid sharing a bed with my father.

Then, one day, in the most unselfish of gestures, you handed me a suitcase, opened the door, and pushed me out, sending me away from you, away from the pain to seek a better life. With your own hands, you condemned yourself, willingly, to the bleak loneliness that would be your main companion for all those years to come.

You freed me.

Or did you?

Sometimes when I called and you were in a good mood, we found comfort in talking about food, one of the only subjects of mutual interest left between us by then. Recalling the old recipes, the hefty Hungarian dishes you used to make—chicken paprika with the handmade *nokedly* noodles, cheese and plum dumplings, cold sour cherry soup, cinnamon pies. On one of your earlier brushes with death, when Monika's long-distance phone call tried to prepare me for the possibility that you might have cancer (you didn't—then), as I exited

Grand Central Station and was crossing Madison Avenue on my way to the office, the thought that I might never again eat your stuffed cabbage brought a sudden flood of tears into my eyes.

I digress. I was telling your story and am about to end up with stuffed cabbage recipes. I try to stall, paralyzed.

My page is almost blank. There is much to tell, yet I don't know what. I couldn't ask. It had been your lifelong goal to shield me from this story and I didn't dare change the rules we have so carefully decreed and followed. So I arrange and rearrange the few hints I have painstakingly collected, trying to somehow illuminate the interiors of this Pandora's box. I am terrified to find out what it holds. To discover that, in fact, its contents are already firmly implanted in me, sprouting from my visage. All I have to do is look in the mirror.

It is now *my* turn to remember. I am your safe-keeper. Unbeknown to us, a secret transfusion has occurred. A wordless transmission of information between hub and spoke. An inheritance of memories that started in your womb, sending tiny, steady molecules via the placenta. The echo of screams that resonated in your bloodstream was registered in my neural pathways, nails scratched, seeking outlet, leaving their mark on the walls of my forming organs, and an unspeakable, bottomless agony took permanent possession to be residing in my cells, spreading like venom, filling every opening.

I became a vessel. A carrier. A holder. A container.

I became a monument that they had existed.

I became a vehicle to move in between. Then and now. There and here. And back there.

I became a transgenerational spaceship. A rope connecting past and present.

I became their tool. Their voice.

I am on duty. To remind. To accuse. To prevent healing.

I am your witness. I'll be your mouth to speak for you when you are no longer. I do not know the words. Yet I am your only witness. And even without names or photos, without ever having seen the faces, the places. I know the end. Of what was and is no more.

I am not a worthy witness, but I am the only one left. Who wasn't there but still remembers. There was a place on the banks of a river, raspberries climbing on a fence, bread (not children) baking in the oven, serenades under your window playing to your vanity. A woman who didn't live to know I'd be her granddaughter. There was a world.

I am their witness.

Dundaga

Near Riga, Latvia, 1944

No one ever heard of Dundaga. We all know about Auschwitz, of course, Dachau, Buchenwald, Treblinka, Bergen Belsen, Majdanek. Those are the "famous" concentration/death camps. But the actual list goes on and on. My internet search yielded a generous bounty of thousands of camps and sub-camps—an industry exceeding any other; the vast majority of its "factories" are obscure, meaningless names for us. As if the murder of Jews below a critical mass of, say, a hundred thousand, is not even worth calling attention to. Dundaga was but a tiny dot in that universe.

You did not mention it either. The name never crossed your lips, at least not in my presence. I had to wait until after your death. I had to wait until you were no longer able to protect me from the knowledge. I had to call your sister Sari— her raspy voice reaching me from the other end of the line in Williamsburg, Brooklyn—to hear it for the first time.

Miraculously, you and your two sisters managed to stay together during deportation. Thanks to Sari's canny knack for survival and endless coincidences defying all statistics, you, a lucky by-product, endured as well. She was the one who managed to land, in one of the camps you were marched to, in a coveted position in the vegetable garden. She sneaked out carrots, turnips, and potatoes, was caught, beaten until she lost the sight in one of her eyes, and continued sneaking out carrots, turnips, and potatoes the following day as if nothing had happened. That meager prize she shared with you. You told me about the incident and, fifty years later, your voice still conveyed disbelief at your sister's dumb stubbornness and courage. But not a word about Dundaga.

I had to wait.

You are gone, and I finally ask. It is time to search for this piece of the puzzle and insert it in its proper place. I stretch out a hesitant finger and touch the curtain that veils the "black hole"—that forbidden year. Secreted, it nevertheless accompanied me like a shadow for as long as I can remember. I fear the findings, all that general knowledge about the "Holocaust" turning into real dates and places. Turning into what was done to *you*. Into places I was at with you, albeit hiding within the folds of your then young body. Where I shared your fast heartbeats, panic, confusion, my tiny molecular existence depending on the hazards that determined yours.

I breach what was a lifelong taboo and it feels almost obscene. My lips hesitate to form the questions. But the investigation turns out to be surprisingly easy. All that was prohibited, words that were unmentionable, become plain facts.

Sari lists the camps almost enthusiastically, as if she had been waiting for someone to finally ask. Next, your friend Magda dedicates a whole morning to telling me the sequence of events. As Elise and I sit in her living room, a tape recorder resting on the coffee table next to a plate of irresistible *zserbo* cakes (Magda's specialty), she is talking. She talks, uninterrupted, for two long hours. You are no longer around to censor the contents.

The war was almost over; D-Day was a few weeks into the future, and the Russian troops were fighting and gaining ground in Moldavia.

On May 3, 1944, came the order to move to the ghetto—a former brick factory.

The last mass human transport left Hungary to Auschwitz on July 8, 1944.

The whole operation took no more than ten weeks. Half a million Hungarian Jews were deported. One in ten would come back. None of the children. The crematoriums were working at a pace of twelve thousand bodies a day. Only a couple of months separated between life-as-usual and what one can't even call by name—our language is incapable of catching up with human imagination when it comes to devising and carrying out acts of atrocity.

I started reading some testimonies of the few survivors from your ghetto and couldn't bring myself to continue. The torture, sadism of the guards, suffering, glee of your former-neighbors-turned-enthusiastic-spectators are too much to take in, even sitting in the comfort of my well-heated study. Those were my family's last weeks. Did they know?

The four-day train ride to Auschwitz-Birkenau—you were on the second transport to leave the Somnyo Ghetto. Magda tells us she never met anyone from the first or third transports who survived; the whole trainloads, possibly, were sent directly to the gas chambers or the open fire pits that were dug up to manage the overflow. The deportees from Northern Transylvania were too numerous for the "usual" methods of extermination to suffice.

You didn't know any of that when you arrived at the ramp and were greeted by emaciated figures in striped rags. You assumed they were some lunatics and ignored their attempts to warn the young mothers, telling them to let go of the children, to send them off with the elderly grandmothers who were doomed anyway. Piri, my father's younger sister, arriving at about the same time from the Szatmar ghetto, must have been whispered the same warnings but clung to her baby. No, one can't find comfort even in the pitiful notion that she embraced little Roby during their final minutes of agony. The little ones were snatched away from the arms of their mothers and thrown above the adults' heads, cramming even more victims per round of exterminations. Or else, if directed to the open fire pits, they were tossed in alive, not worth wasting a bullet on. Which was my aunt and cousin's fate?

Mengele. With a slight motion of his finger, he directed your mother, sister Erzsi, and young brothers to the left. At forty-two, suffering from a heart ailment, the grandmother I would never know collapsed while standing in line, a few steps ahead of the chamber designed for her murder. Watching her from afar was as close as you'd ever come to saying goodbye. A few moments before, Erzsi, wanting to be with her sisters, sneaked over to the shorter line, refusing her mother's pleas to stay and help with the boys. Who was with them when they undressed? Who held the two frightened kids' hands—nine-year-old Willy and seven-year-old Zoli—while gasping their last scorched breaths?

Not one day has gone by without asking myself those questions.

Loaded again, onto cargo trains. The three sisters and a randomly chosen group of five hundred women were sent east, to a camp near Riga, Latvia. Hold. This is a detail I do recognize. You did mention Riga. We once passed by a group of men working at a road construction site. You pointed at the heavy machinery they were using to dig holes in the asphalt and said, "That's what I did in Riga."

I was little at the time and could not believe that my mom, with her sickly constitution, had held a machine that seemed to shake even the muscular, sweaty men operating it. It did not seem credible, but you ignored my follow-up questions. You had already revealed more than you intended to.

Drill. Riga. Jews were used as slave labor to build roads for the German marching troops. The pieces start fitting together. Like a detective, I try to retrace your steps based on little hints you stingily volunteered, information I dug up from books, and now, these firsthand accounts. Transported from camp to camp to the orders of a random, chaotic, and incomprehensible force.

"From Riga, we were transferred to Dundaga," continues Aunt Sari. "I don't want to talk about Dundaga."

It is Magda who tells me that you were given twenty lashes—the guard deemed you were "lazy," taking a momentary repose from mining the frozen ground. Your friends dragged your broken body to the barracks and nursed you back to life.

When the Russian army was closing in, you were so frightened by the incessant bombardments that your sisters had to hold you down to stop you from screaming and drawing the German guards' attention; you jeopardized them all with your cowardice.

Transported again, by boats—some sinking on the way, but who cared—to Stutthof. Then Gloven—where, despite the evident outcome of the war, the torture continued for an additional six months. Luckily, the conditions in that subcamp were relatively "good," with only one death, of typhus—not gas, not beating, not executions, none of the many other forms in which death was the nonchalant rule rather than the exception—among the women prisoners.

"Can you imagine it?" Magda repeats, her voice still incredulous. "Five hundred inmates and only one died!"

Magda was an avid reader and excellent student. When the order came, she carried her schoolbooks with her to the ghetto, hoping to take the end-of-the-year exams as soon as the war was over. You met each other standing in line, waiting for the first "selection" under Mengele's gaze. A few hours later, Magda and her sixteen-year-old sister were each other's only family; the rest had been reduced to dust. When the Germans called for experienced dental assistants, the sister raised her hand, hoping that being "useful" would provide some protection from imminent death. After all, their mother's last words were, "Take care of Magda, she is so very young!"

It was not the living who needed dental care.

"People told me they saw her toward the end of the war in Stutthof. She was still alive but wouldn't talk to anyone. Pulling gold teeth from corpses' mouths was not an experience she could recover from." Magda is silent for a moment. "No one could tell me what happened to her afterward. I can't but blame myself. My sister sacrificed her life in order to protect me."

The guilt of the innocent.

At fourteen, Edith, strikingly beautiful with her long black curls, stood out even in the crowd of thousands awaiting selection. Noticing the German guard circling her and fearing his intentions, the older women took advantage of his momentary departure to swiftly cut Edith's hair, making her indistinguishable from the rest. Standing right behind, you tried to console the sobbing girl for the loss of her locks, the first of far greater demises.

All three—Edith, Magda, and you—ended up in that "fortunate" group of five hundred. You'd remain friends for life, sustaining each other through bad marriages, divorces, endless card games, bitter disputes and emotional reconciliations, illnesses, and now your death.

Back to Stutthof and another march. Herded west at gunpoint, you were chased away from the promise of liberty that one could almost touch but was exceedingly hopeless to reach alive. Any of the living dead lagging behind or falling were stamped on by hundreds of desperately marching feet; the air was vibrating with the sound of shots, and a thickening trail of bodies marked your path in the snow. You shared with me a useful "technique" you learned on that march: as you were walking in rows of five, arms linked, you took turns changing places so that the three in the center could sleep while still walking blindly, the two on each side awake, pulling the row forward. Gives sleepwalking a whole new meaning. It finally ended in a forest near the Elbe River. Again, it was Sari's resourcefulness that saved your lives. First by not letting you climb onto the wagon assigned for those who could no longer walk—tempted by the illusion of rest, they were summarily shot. Then by pulling you into a ditch by the side of the road. You stayed under the cover of darkness and confusion, awaiting the arrival of the Russian troops, while the column of walking corpses continued.

"As random luck would have it," continued Magda, "there were two Jewish officers among the Russians, with whom we could communicate in Yiddish."

Their strict warning to move only at night and avoid other Russians at all cost saved you from the gang rapes that were the fate of some other survivors.

* *

Decades later, the pupils in Elise's class would be asked by Mrs. Church, the third-grade teacher, to "interview" their grandparents for a project designed to explore each family's roots. The resulting "family trees" were to be displayed in the school hallways. The kids were given a questionnaire with a list of queries to pose. We called you. Going down the list, we reached an innocent enough question:

"Who was your best friend when you were in elementary school?"

"Ildiko. We were in the same class and sat next to each other for six years."

Elise proceeded to the next question:

"What was she like? Can you describe her?"

"I don't want to talk about her. When the war ended and we were already on our way home, the train stopped and Ildiko got off to pee. She was noticed by a group of about fifty Russian soldiers, and when they were done with her, she was dead."

I didn't translate your answer. Every benign recollection conceals a minefield waiting to explode. How does one live, raise children—children who go on a sleepover with their "best friend"—when the shadow of your own childhood playmate being raped and torn to pieces is imprinted in your brain cells?

Sanity seems like a mental deformation.

Magda's eyes brighten with joy as her husband walks in. He is your age—you grew up in the same village—tall, his back straight, a broad, sunny smile reveals what must be perfect dentures.

"You are the spitting image of your mother," he says, somewhat surprised.

Last time he saw me, I must have been Elise's age. It's summer, and he is wearing a short-sleeved shirt. I am so used to seeing it that I don't even notice, but Elise is shaken by the blue number tattooed onto his arm. I can feel her withdrawing in her seat next to me.

"He survived," his wife explains, "cleaning latrines, alternating between transporting loads of excrement and loads of corpses in a wheelbarrow. Nowadays," she continues in clear amusement, "he has become an impossible aesthete who won't eat in a restaurant unless he is satisfied with its cleanliness. I often tease him, asking whether he acquired his squeamishness in Auschwitz."

She laughs as she puts her arms around her husband's neck and plants a kiss on his lips. Growing up, I never witnessed such a loving relationship between my parents.

Soon after the war, to rid themselves of her care, Magda was quickly married off by some distant relatives to a man twenty-five years her senior. Not that different from your fate. By nineteen, a mother of two, she rebelled, left, and remarried the man she loved. Broken to pieces and patched back together again, Magda and Henrik created a miracle. Among all your acquaintances—families hastily formed to replace the void of the parted—they were the only couple I knew to find true comfort and delight in each other. No wonder you envied her so. The contentment she eventually achieved attested to courage you never possessed. You were never brave enough to salvage your life and reclaim your own happiness. Perhaps that was the reason you kept silent throughout all those years while Magda was able to talk. She freed herself from the curse. You remained locked in it. You didn't have the resilience—which requires a certain hardheartedness—to leave your dead ones behind. There was no one to fill the hollowness they left.

The Drowned. None Saved.

In me, ad infinitum

With these accounts, names, places finally in hand, I continue the research.

I search for Dundaga on the internet. All I find on Wikipedia is more or less as follows: "Dundaga is a village in Courland, Latvia. It is famous for its castle from the late thirteenth century, constructed by the Archbishopric of Riga. From the sixteenth until the twentieth century, Dundaga Castle was the centre of the largest private estate in Courtland. Dundaga Castle is connected with many fairy tales and legends." Fairy tales and legends. Nothing about concentration camps.

I learn a bit more in *The Murder of the Jews in Latvia 1941–1945.*[1] Apparently, hardly any detailed descriptions exist about Dundaga concentration camp simply because there were so few survivors. The inmates received a slice of bread in the morning and watery soup in the evening,

---

1 Bernhard Press, *The Murder of the Jews in Latvia 1941–1945* (Evanston, IL: Northwestern University Press, 2000).

living in tents of pressed cardboard that were sunk into the ground. The Germans built a giant training camp for tanks in Dundaga using prisoners, including several thousand Hungarian Jewish women brought from Auschwitz, for the construction effort. The work consisted of clearing the forest and, since it was beyond the strength of the "workers," the Germans and kapos beat and murdered them for whatever reason. The Hungarian Jewish women could not tolerate the physical exertion and the abominable living conditions and faced daily selections.

I am reminded that you did mention the food portions, showing me the tip of your little finger to demonstrate:

"This is the size of the margarine we got each morning. This, and watery coffee. And then there was the *Appell*. At times, during the daily roll call, they would pick those standing at places that were multiples of ten—all prisoners numbered ten, twenty, thirty . . . twenty-five twenty . . . and so on—to be sent to the gas chambers. Once, when I ended up in such a place, Sari pushed me aside and stood there in my stead."

Luckily—for Sari but not for those taken—on that occasion the selection was based on other criteria. No wonder even my hardened aunt prefers to forget.

I follow your route. Information is easier to find about your next station—Stutthof. As Soviet forces approached in July and August of 1944, Jews from forced-labor camps in the occupied Baltic States were evacuated by sea to the Stutthof concentration camp.

Gloven—must have been too small to be worth mentioning. An internet search produces but two references. One is an account written by an American girl about the war experiences of her Transylvanian-born grandmother. Probably a school project, like Elise's. Again, the article mentions the grandmother being one of the providential five hundred picked for labor at the Gloven camp in Latvia. The second is a testimony dated January 1996 and entitled "From Sachsenhausen to the 'Belower Wald'" written by Joseph Rotbaum-Ribo about his arrival at Gloven. "The camp consisted of four long huts which served as our lodgings and a small one for toilets and showers. Next to our camp was a camp with Jewish women prisoners from Hungary. The two camps were separated by a fence of reeds in addition to the barbed-wire fence. Most of our guards were elderly SS-men, and the treatment we received here was much milder in comparison to Sachsenhausen. What we suffered from most was the cold and hunger."

You, too, mentioned an elderly German guard who turned a blind eye when there was no one else around. Fearful for his own safety, he would scold you to resume work only when his fellow guards approached. You still remembered gratefully the one person treating you like human beings, even calling you *meine Kinder*, my children. Indeed, it was a "good camp." There are five hundred thousand untold stories of torture and death for every five hundred hand-picked miracles of survival. And due to the scarcity of miracles, this story of the five hundred is one of the few that can be recycled over and over to give an illusion that there was hope in that darkness.

Growing up in Israel, the Holocaust Memorial Day was solemnly commemorated every year. It was not, however, a day to commemorate *our* family and *your* experience. In those days, it had little to do with what you went through. It was called "the Holocaust and Bravery Memorial Day," with the emphasis on the latter. The story of the revolt of the Warsaw Ghetto was told over and over again. The Israelis liked that story—"the few who fought with their bare hands against tanks, humbling the mighty German army, bringing it to its knees for weeks until the heroic death of the last fighter." That story was worth being told. Yours—"marching obediently like lamb to the slaughter"—was not. You and your sort were condemned to silence while the country was cultivating a new species of life form—a proud Jew. Above all, one that would carry no resemblance to you. I grew up ashamed of my parents, neither heroic nor brave. In a country that for perhaps justified reasons idolized heroism, you were an undesirable "souvenir."

I grew up with your shame. Inhaling with the air surrounding me the shame of those who survived—for having survived, for having "deserted" those who didn't, failing to rescue or go with them, letting them die. Often, shame for what had to be done in order to live. How did your cousin, Judith, justify her own struggle to survive when her seven-year-old, Adi, was handed over to an elderly family member?

Was she ever able to love the second Adi, born after the war to replace the first, or did guilt sabotage any emotion?

The shame of the victim.

I inherited that shame. Because no matter how much I try to concentrate on, identify with, accompany my lost family—I still abandon them in their loneliness, suffering, devastation, fear, hideous end. I leave them behind in a past that cannot be undone. Far less deserving, I am allowed to continue my trivial existence. My daughters' eyes are filled with plans, hope, inspiration, enthusiasm, and ideas that they'd have a lifetime to realize. Surely *theirs* were not less passionate . . . yet those dreams expired with them. The happiest event in my aunt Piri's life, the birth of her son, condemned her, only nine months later, to death; it deprived her of whatever slim chance she would have had to survive. In what way do we merit this random luck—to live, while they didn't?

Night after night, I am trying to escape. To shut my eyes, my ears, my sense of smell, my angst (what if it happens again? where do I go?), my doubts (would I love my daughters enough to stay with them rather than save myself, if I could?), my hatred (why did I shake that German colleague's hand and smile in such a friendly way?), my helplessness (why don't I have the courage to avenge?).

I abhor the people who tell me, "You should let go. It all happened so long ago . . ."

Perhaps well-meaning, they can't fathom how much their futile advice hurts. How it only reveals their complete lack of understanding. How it further entrenches the unbridgeable divide between us. How can I let go? How can I leave Piri and Roby, Willy and Zoli to their lonely oblivion? How can I betray them? Every moment I forget them, they are a little more . . . dead. I fight every day a desperate battle to keep them with me. In me. In the only space they still occupy in this world.

History books conclude that "the Allies won the war." The existence of the State of Israel is a "triumph." Holocaust Memorial Day articles in newspapers quote survivors pointing to their children and numerous grandchildren as living proof of our "victory." Others recount stories of survival and credit their intense desire to live—as if those who perished had somehow "failed" that test. They mention the words "courage" and "bravery" as if those who perished had been less courageous. Or resourceful. Or smart. We love to hear those remarkable stories—the "hero" who, one out of a thousand, defying all odds, "won." It has a Hollywood sort of magnetism. It satisfies a certain primal need in us. We don't want to hear about the nine hundred ninety-nine out of the thousand who, succumbing to the odds, didn't.

In reality, neither the Germans nor fate much cared how desperately one wanted or "deserved" to live. More likely, the finest were first to lose in a universe that was based on brute power and encouraged ruthless struggle for a slice of bread. Though our psyche is unable to deal with the "defeated," the non-heroes—they were the rule, not the exception. We turn anecdotes into the main narrative. But that is a lie. An illusion we blind ourselves with. The main stories are those we do *not* hear, that no one is left to tell.

This is the raw truth:

The Allies did *not* win the war. They did not win the war for nine-month-old Roby or my aunt Piri. Nor for seven-year-old Zoli or for nine-year-old Willie. Not for my uncle Sandor nor for his fiancée, Lili. Not for my aunt Margit, not for my aunt Sara, not for my grandma Esther, not for my grandma Regina, not for my grandfather Herman, not for the babies whose heads were smashed against stone walls or tree trunks, not for the children crushed under the weight of bodies in the gas chambers, not for those who were waiting in the snow for days to be shot and dumped into ditches and ravines, not for those locked in synagogues and burnt alive, not for . . . how many volumes would it take just to note down the methods, let alone the names of those murdered? For them—no matter how strong their desire to live may have been—the war was lost in 1941, 1942, 1943, 1944, or even one day before or after the formal declaration of German surrender in May of 1945. For them, spring never came. For them, the war was absolutely, conclusively, undeniably, and without a doubt . . . lost.

And with your family dead, your youth destroyed, your hopes shattered, your nights forever pierced by nightmares—wasn't the war lost for you too?

Instead of the BC/AD dating system, my timeline is divided by the deportation of the Hungarian Jews: BEFORE May 1944—and AFTER. Those born BEFORE are guilty. Buildings erected BEFORE are guilty. Parks planted BEFORE are guilty. Carousels that revolved BEFORE are guilty. All who existed BEFORE and looked on should tear out their eyeballs and die of shame.

I search and search and will never come one iota closer to understanding. I can't add "color" to the events narrated above. I can't make it "show," not "tell," as taught in writing courses. I read accounts about "secrets" that survivors' descendants have discovered years after the Holocaust. All those stories trying to give some heroic meaning, mystic significance, excitement to the events. I despise that voyeurism. That artificially infused spectacle. No, there are no "secrets" in this story. No "revelations" in hindsight. There is no need to dramatize the horror of what happened; it speaks for itself. I didn't "discover" anything that was not known already. The plain, same, repeated and repeated and repeated and repeated and repeated and repeated and repeated and repeated and repeated and repeated, six million times repeated story—your parents and young brothers were gassed and then burnt. Ignorant of the fact that you'd never see them again, you couldn't even say a last goodbye; that confused, frenzied separation was for eternity. You had been missing them with every breath since. It's simple. I can't see those images other than in the black and white of documentaries. I don't know what Dundaga looked like. I can't "make up" a literary description of the camp. I can't "imagine" the stink of eighty people defecating in a locked wagon. Nor the smell of burning bodies. I can't feel hunger that is longer than missing a meal. I never experienced cold that was not covered with a warm coat or blanket.

Most importantly, I can't sense the *fear*. The kind that makes one lose control of their bowels. It can't be conveyed in words. It happens in a very different part of our brain. Once imprinted, it cannot be erased. You were never again without it. It existed in you until your last breath. Miraculously, though, that fear did not survive you in me. It was the one element barred from passing the placenta in our two-way transfusion. Your one glorious success in "protecting" me and the only battle you actually *won*.

But I am *your* daughter. One of your cells. My heart learned to beat at the tune of yours—and I follow your course. I am unable to adopt Magda's healthy resolution. For me, happiness will always feel like a crime. All I can do, at best, is continue my existence as a vessel to your memories. Faithful to your inheritance, I wait, am vigilant; collecting passports, identities, temporary homes. And I never board a train without remembering what could be its final destination. The only lesson I learned from my failed attempt to tell your story is that life and death and luck and pain are all

   random, random, random.

My mission is over. I can't do better. The puzzle will forever remain incomplete. And the blank gaps will continue expending like black ink stains, sucking me into a paralyzing bleakness.

* *

And once a year, on Yom Kippur, I go to synagogue to con-
front a God I don't believe in. Like a schizophrenic, I am
drawn in and then reject Him. As the members of the congre-
gation recite the prayers—"Oh, Merciful Lord"—I fight the
urge to spit my rage in His face and leave in revolt. Only my
tears are holding me back. Elise is by my side.

"Mommy, why are you crying?"

"I cry for my family. For those who are dead."

"Why here?"

"There is no other place, so I cry here."

"Don't they have graves?"

"No, they don't."

"Why not?"

Session 28

Epitaph

Israel, April 30, 2014

Four months to the day after your death. Visiting Israel, your grave, the few friends who outlived you, I am immersed in the process of erasing your life. The little electric "scooter" you were so proud of—sporting black sunglasses, a leather jacket, your white hair blowing in the wind as you maneuvered it expertly, ignoring traffic rules, speeding past cars, an eighty-six-year-old "Mad Max"; you referred to it as your "motorcycle," taking no notice of its geriatric purposes—is sold first. The contract for the sale of the apartment you so painstakingly decorated is executed at the lawyer's offices; the furniture is called for by one acquaintance or another. I sold the fridge, the washing machine and dryer, the two little nightstands, the electric kettle, the plates and silverware and canned food—all for a trifle. Whatever else is unclaimed by the neighbors will be given away or dumped in the green garbage container in front of the building. The buyer of the apartment said he would see to emptying the place. He is planning extensive renovations and I am glad not to bear witness to the sights of destruction and rebuilding. I want to remember your kingdom just the way you left it.

I am guilt-ridden to so quickly purge all that was so dear to you and in awe at how fast it all gets done, as if on its own. I feel as if I am burying you for a second time. As if I am betraying your trust. You wanted me to safeguard your memory, and I wipe it out. Soon there will be nothing left of you—not a wall, not a bed, not a pot in your kitchen. Other than your image in front of my eyes and your voice in my ears, my face in the mirror, my gestures, the things I do and what I say that have come eerily to resemble yours. I, who have become you.

And one of two adjacent, very simple tombstones, with your name freshly engraved on it.

Lost

Nowhere, Late 2014

Has it been almost a year?

But you are still alive in me. Or am I dead with you?

I have trouble reconciling your very live image in my mind with the dead waxy face I identified at the cemetery. It had no more to do with you than the yellowing, plucked chicken I bought in the market, wrapped in a kitchen towel and put in the fridge. Dead protein.

Has it been almost a year?

I pass by the hotel you stayed in on your last visit to Paris. The window of your room facing the street stares at me. I gaze back accusingly—does the room still remember?

As I rummage through a bag I usually carry with me on overseas trips, I discover a five-hundred euro note. It's a souvenir from our ritual. Every visit, before my departure, you'd insert a bunch of bills into my wallet or pocketbook. I'd usually discover the money soon enough, put it in a cabinet drawer or under the cover of the piano keyboard, and later call from the airport to let you know where I had placed it. That failed, symbolic gesture gave you an illusion of still "taking care" of me. This last note must have escaped my detection. I now have the eerie sense that you are able to place gifts in my bag even from beyond the boundaries of life.

I see in front of my eyes the picture of you greedily eating ice cream just a few days before the end. The cold sensation seemed to, at least temporarily, quench your bottomless thirst. I averted my eyes so as not to embarrass you, wanting to let you enjoy what in hindsight I realize was your last meal—in private. With stubborn determination, you dug again and again into the soft cream, scooping spoonful after spoonful in utter gluttony, slowly bringing the spoon to your toothless mouth, your parched tongue stretched out in anticipation. I was worried you might make yourself sick, but then gave up and left the room. A couple of spoonfuls later you stopped. I am now ashamed by my reluctance to allow you that last dismal joy.

It's autumn again, and the smell of roasting chestnuts meets me on almost every street corner. I don't think I will ever be able to eat chestnuts without a nudging sense of guilt for having them without you.

With a sudden jolt, I realize that I forgot to say, "Thank you for all you did for me" before you parted. Too late.

Endless regrets.

For giving you a pill to doze off—you missed a few hours of living.

For opting to wait instead of an immediate burial. I

should not have left your body in the morgue from Friday until Sunday. Perhaps you were cold?

Has it been a year?

I start, just ever so slightly, neglecting myself. Letting the gray sneak out of my hair. Letting the lipstick fade without reapplying it. I notice a new wrinkle and a bit of sagging around the jaw line.

I feel your blood on my hands, as if I killed you or at least hastened your death. Please forgive me, Mama (I know you do). I didn't have a choice and we both knew it.

I can't redo your death. Learn from my mistakes and correct them. Do better next time. It was a one-time opportunity. Unique performance. It's done. And it's irreversible.

I should seek professional help. But I don't. Even the pain is better than losing your presence entirely.

I prepare coffee. We bought the perfumed beans together, in a village en route to Jerusalem—not knowing that when I'd brew them into coffee, you would no longer be with us. Once all the beans are used, one more piece of our life together will be forever gone.

Every time I sit in a café watching the sunset, as we did on that magical afternoon by the sea, I feel the sting of a mini-death.

Mia sends me an angry email, ending with: "I never want to see you again." I tear up. Not because of what she writes, which would soon be forgotten. I cry because I know that when I am gone, she'll miss me the way I miss you. She'll experience this bottomless pain and regret. I wish I could somehow save her from it, but I can't.

Passover again. I am on a short visit to Israel. On my way to a Seder dinner with friends, I make a quick stop. The parking lot is deserted. My rental car is the only yellow dot in a sea of asphalt. The gate is shut, but when I push, it yields to the pressure with a rusty squeak. The main square is empty of the habitual mourners, beggars, wailers, prayers, attendants, funerals. I take the wrong path and, for a moment, can't find you. Confused, I look around; no one in sight to ask for directions. I stumble around, lost in a white maze of tombstones, panic gripping my throat. Where are you? Blinded by the still bright rays of a setting sun, I zigzag in between the rows and alleys, my feet tripping on the arid terrain before I face the simple stone with your name carved on it. We are all alone. The air doesn't stir. A bird doesn't squeal. The universe is still. In the silence that engulfs us, I tell you it won't be long before I join you wherever you are.

Has it been over a year?

Session 30
MRI

Paris, January 2015

That nagging pain in my arm and antsy sensation. I dismiss it. I wait, and it won't go away. I have too much time on my hands, so I go to see a specialist. The pain stems from my right shoulder, more precisely the neck, even higher up, below my ear. Dr. Debois prescribes an MRI. I tell myself that it's a routine overreaction, typical of a healthcare system supported by the generous taxpayer. It's silly, a total waste of time. Yet I obey. I call a cab, reach a modern facility off the Champs-Elysées, register, fill out some forms—no allergies, no heart problems, no metal implants—and settle down with my book. I wait. Not for long. Medical treatment is the one area where the French are uncharacteristically efficient. I am called in and asked to undress from the waist up and remove all accessories. I leave my clothes, shoes, watch, necklace, rings, even my cell phone in the antechamber. I put on the paper slippers and gown, adjust the headphone I am handed over my ears, and step toward the massive machine that gaps its cylindrical mouth open for me. I lie on the flat surface and place my hands on my chest. The nurse forewarns me to expect funny noises and that I should not be alarmed. As soon as the door is shut behind her, the device pulls its tongue, swallowing me into its bowels. The rhythmical sound of hammering, growling, and humming emitted from its guts reminds me of the experimental music concerts Elise used to drag me to. It is soothing in its own way, lulling me into a peaceful torpor. Suddenly, the tempo takes on a very different, hurried pace and I find myself down at your feet that are flapping back and forth, moving the pedal of the old Singer sewing machine, and I hear the *clack, clack, clack* rapid stitches chasing each other, piercing the cloth with the needle as you are seaming the prayer shawls in our rented apartment in the suburbs of Tel Aviv. I am again your child. The speedy beat is replaced by calm rustles echoing through walls of liquid substance. A gentle current carries me. I slowly swim, swing, turn, glide as if on waves of a shallow pond. The soft movements calm my embryonic cells. I hear a murmur and recognize it as your heartbeat. I am secure, cuddled in your womb. Just then I am startled by loud thuds. The motions of a mechanical drill shake my body in violent reverberations and I hear dogs barking, see their teeth threatening to tear my flesh apart. I smell the stench of fear, the cold and fatigue penetrate my existence. I hear the noise of boots crushing the icy snow, the orders pronounced in a German staccato, a shot resonates nearby. A cry. A fall. I am hiding in the folds of your ovaries somewhere near Riga. Helpless. Trembling in you. With you. I reached far enough to be reunited with you.

The door opens. It's over.

"You should get dressed and take a seat in the reception area," the nurse announces in a high-pitched, cheerful tone.

This time I wait for a long while.

A door opens and a tall, grave-looking figure signals for me to go in. The slides showing the insides of my head are highlighted on the big screen in front of us on a background of white, fluorescent-like light. I am far from being interested; this is not my field. I can't decipher any of the images. They all look like some abstract modern art with white and dark areas splashed in irregular shapes. The doctor is obviously hesitant, perhaps searching for the right word in English so that this "American" patient can understand. He takes awhile before he starts talking. His voice is calm, his eyes compassionate. He is a handsome man. His lips are moving while he absent-mindedly rubs the stubble on his left cheek. I follow his mouth as it rounds up, the muscles relax, then round up again, his head tilts a bit to the side. I notice he has a straight and beautiful nose, in a manly way. His finger points to a dark spot on the slides, his gaze is focused on it. He avoids meeting my eyes, and as he speaks, I hear the faint shadow of your voice calling—or is it my longing for you that is confusing me? It dawns on me that I may have been secretly hoping to meet you again sooner than expected, that it may now be my turn to move along the corridor toward the exit sign. The monotonous voice goes on, the finger scrawls circles on my skull that is reflected on the screen. He watches carefully for my reaction, but I no longer pay attention. He must be saying that he will be sending the results, together with his recommendations, to my physician. For a moment, I stare blankly at him then collect myself, return his handshake, offer a smile that is not reciprocated—French doctors tend to be more pompous than friendly—and part with a brown manila envelope full of slides under my arm.

Since you are gone, I was trying to learn how to die. I have been practicing a little every day. I see the road ahead winding into the horizon. Are you there, waiting for me? The thought is mildly surprising, yet strangely comforting. And in the blur that follows, I laugh and let go.

Session 31
Round and Round We Go

W hat can I bequeath to you, my little ones, besides a closet full of clothes and five hundred pairs of shoes, far too small for your growing feet? Not much in the form of material achievements, no trust fund, no portfolio of stocks and debt instruments. I dealt with lots of those in my professional life but failed miserably in accumulating any for my own account. When I tried "investing," I made all the wrong decisions, buying when the market was high, selling when it was low. No, not much to offer there. Each of you already manages her pocket money better than I did the family fortunes. Money, in and of itself, never represented anything to me in the sense of wanting to accumulate it. Shoes did. Forget it. Nothing to learn from me on that front.

Love? Relationships? Same. Always on the wrong end of the investment scheme. No great achievements to present. But at least I was having fun while I was at it—other than when I was miserable, of course. And I was quite addicted to the game. Sorry, no useful lessons to be learned from me on that front either.

What else? I may be better off concluding with a blank page here. But, just as in music, the pauses are as important as the notes, and the bare page is as important as the one filled with words. That is the most important message I have for you—the lack of message, of recipe, of instructions, of agenda. You will have enough room to write your own story. What better gift could a mother offer?

Carve out your own road, learn your own lessons—do not accept them from me or anyone else. Write your judgments and then modify them as you go along. Kick every holy cow no matter how fat she is. Never adhere to any diet, doctrine, dogma, truth. Stay away from prophets, from those who know, those who tell you they know—above all, from those who believe.

From time to time, take your hand and insert it into your chest, searching for that steel ball I planted between your breastbone and your diaphragm. I planted it through years of kisses, feeding you my love, telling you how beautiful you are, yelling at you to do your homework and practice your violin or cello. By now that ball is harder than any substance in the universe. You are indestructible.

Just like my mother did before me, I only know how to protect my children from the dangers of the past that may no longer be relevant. There are new ones lurking in the shadows and even in plain view. How do I equip you to take on these new dangers? I have been collecting passports to protect you from another bloodthirsty dictator, but a mountain of those may not be of any use against the perils you may encounter. I have only my love to offer. To bury it deep, inside your young bodies, so that I can accompany you even after my death—my strength and hers before me and back to all those mothers we never knew—all accumulated within you; and we never die, we live forever within you, for you, for us.

What a burden to carry! What a curse—a never dying mother—always inside your guts, never to be rid of. I imitate my own monster of a mother. I went too far. Got carried away. Sorry. I leave. I free you from my love. That is a bigger gift than love.

We were a triangle. I told you a triangle was the strongest structure in the universe—whether or not that is scientifically true, I never bothered to check. Making things up is one of the privileges of motherhood. I grew up in a close, suffocating, poisonous but protective triangle with my parents and then I created my own—the three of us. Once I am gone, you must invent your own forms of geometry. Don't be afraid to be creative.

The Jewish legend tells us that babies come into this world with their hands curled into fists, as if saying, "The whole world is in my hands."

We depart with our hands stretched flat: "I exit empty-handed. I have not taken anything from this world."

When you were little girls, each in her turn, you still liked to listen to Mommy singing, not minding how out of tune I was. At the end of a day full of play or anguish, I used to lie in bed right next to you, imitating her while caressing your manes of dark hair, whispering in your ears the Yiddish lullaby she used to sing to me. The same one her mother sang to her, and on and on even before any of them reached the banks of the *Szomos* river as they marched from one nowhere to the next, putting centuries of little girls to bed while carrying forward—"*Shluf, shluf, mein taiere meidale. Mach shoyn tzi theim taiere oygale. Ay, lu lu lu lu lu. Ay, lu lu lu lu. Ay, lu lu lu lu . . .*"

I thought this story would end with her death.

I was wrong.

Epigenetics*

The study of heritable changes that occur without a change in the DNA sequence.

(Assorted definitions)

It is clear that at least some epigenetic modifications are heritable, passed from parents to offspring in a phenomenon that is generally referred to as epigenetic inheritance, or passed down through multiple generations via transgenerational epigenetic inheritance. The mechanism by which epigenetic information is inherited is unclear.[2]

Epigenetics even hints that we can . . . inherit biological memories of what our mothers and fathers (or grandmothers and grandfathers) ate and breathed and endured . . . Epigenetic changes live on in cells and their descendants.[3]

Children of mothers who suffered post traumatic stress disorder (PTSD) as a result of the Holocaust are more prone to develop PTSD, even though they had no direct experience of the Holocaust. Interestingly, though all children of Holocaust

---

2 "Epigenetics," *Encyclopedia Britannica*, updated May 3, 2023, https://www.britannica.com/science/epigenetics.

3 Sam Kean, *The Violinist's Thumb: And Other Lost Tales of Love, War, and Genius, as Written by Our Genetic Code* (New York: Little, Brown and Company, 2012).

survivors are more prone to depression, second-generation PTSD is only elevated in those whose mothers suffered PTSD; there is no such correlation for children whose fathers experienced PTSD as a result of the Holocaust. This fact suggests an important role for the fetal environment.[4]

---

4 Richard C. Francis, *Epigenetics: The Ultimate Mystery of Inheritance* (New York: W.W. Norton & Company, 2011).

About the Author

Eva Izsak grew up in Israel and graduated from the Hebrew University School of Law. For over twenty years she practiced with some of the largest law firms in New York and served as in-house counsel in the US and in France. A mother of two daughters, Eva lives in Tokyo, Tel Aviv, New York, and Paris.

SELECTED TITLES FROM SHE WRITES PRESS

She Writes Press is an independent publishing company founded to serve women writers everywhere. Visit us at www.shewritespress. com.

When It's Over by Barbara Ridley. $16.95, 978-1-63152-296-3
When World War II envelopes Europe, Lena Kulkova flees Czechoslovakia for the relative safety of England, leaving her Jewish family behind in Prague.

An Address in Amsterdam by Mary Dingee Fillmore.
$16.95, 978-1-63152-133-1
After facing relentless danger and escalating raids for 18 months, Rachel Klein—a well-behaved young Jewish woman who transformed herself into a courier for the underground when the Nazis invaded her country—persuades her parents to hide with her in a dank basement, where much is revealed.

Bess and Frima by Alice Rosenthal. $16.95, 978-1-63152-439-4
Bess and Frima, best friends from the Bronx, find romance at their summer jobs at Jewish vacation hotels in the Catskills—and as love mixes with war, politics, creative ambitions, and the mysteries of personality, they leave girlhood behind them.

Closer to Fine by Jodi S. Rosenfeld. $16.95, 978-1-64742-059-8
Bisexual and Jewish, Rachel Levine must battle the homophobia and misogyny of her own community, and even her own family, while falling in love, coming of age, and developing personally and professionally into the woman she was meant to become.

Even in Darkness by Barbara Stark-Nemon. $16.95, 978-1-63152-956-6
From privileged young German-Jewish woman to concentration camp refugee, Kläre Kohler navigates the horrors of war and—through unlikely sources—finds the strength, hope, and love she needs to survive.